JUGGLING

EVIDENCE

Other legal thrillers by Michael Monhollon

Criminal Intent

Juggling Evidence (Robing Starling #2)

Dog Law (Robin Starling #3)

Guilty Knowledge

A Robin Starling Legal Thriller
Volume 2

JUGGLING
EVIDENCE

Michael Monhollon

Reflection Publishing
Abilene, Texas

ISBN: 0971214239
ISBN-13: 978-0971214231

For Rachel

Chapter 1

The woman who stood when I entered the reception area was wearing sunglasses despite the subdued lighting. The day outside was overcast, too, or had been when I came in, which made the sunglasses even more incongruous. The boy with her was about twenty or so. Though he was a decade younger than I was, his eyes cut downward when he saw me before flicking back up to my face. I don't know what men find so fascinating about a woman's knees, but I've gotten used to it.

"I'm Robin Starling," I said, holding out my hand to the woman.

She took it in a weak grip. "Lynn Nolan. You did some wills and a trust last year for my husband and me." I couldn't see her eyes through the sunglasses, but there was some discoloration on her cheek just visible beneath them. Though she was forty or so, her long, blond hair fell past her shoulders.

"I'm Matt Nolan," the boy said when I looked at him. His dark blond hair was combed roughly forward in bangs that covered his forehead.

"Come on back," I said.

I led them down the hall to my glass-walled office. I closed the door to give us auditory privacy, but at the law firm of Northcutt, Hambrick and Larsen, visual privacy was something denied to associate attorneys and their clients. The Nolans sat in the client chairs as I walked around my desk. Matt was wearing baggy jeans and a striped polo shirt that looked too small for him. Lynn was wearing capris and a matching jacket over a pale cotton blouse. She was tall, though several inches shorter than I was—maybe five feet six or seven.

"Are you here about your estate planning?" I asked. "Has something changed?"

Lynn Nolan raised her hands to the stems of her sunglasses and took them off.

She had a black eye with some swelling over her cheekbone and a bit of purpling along the lower rim of her eye socket. The contrast with her pale coloring made it look like she was wearing a fright mask.

"Ow," I said.

"I have a question for you."

"Okay."

"Is it possible to get a divorce secretly?"

My eyes slid over to the face of her son Matt. "You mean, are divorces matters of public record? Yes, I'm afraid they are."

"I mean would the person being divorced need to be notified? Or would it be enough for him to find out after the fact?"

"No, he'd have to be notified. A suit for divorce is a lawsuit. Once it's filed, notice and a summons would be served on the other party just as they would be in any lawsuit."

Lynn took a deep breath and let it out slowly. "That's it then," she said. "I was afraid of that."

"That's not it, Mom," Matt said.

"Your husband do this to you?" I asked.

"Last night," Matt said.

"Did you see him do it?" I asked him.

He looked at his mother. "No. I was out. This isn't the first time, though."

"You've seen him hit her before?"

"I've seen him grab her. And hurt her."

I looked at Lynn. "He's hit you before?"

She hesitated, nodded.

"Move out of the house," I said. "We can get a preliminary injunction to keep him away from you while the divorce goes through."

"You don't know Derek."

"Is he home now? We can—"

"He's usually home. He works out of the house."

"Then don't go back. Get what you need at Target and move into a hotel."

She seemed to consider it, then shook her head.

"He keeps close track of her money," Matt said. "He knows exactly how much she's carrying, and she has to account for every cent of it."

"Not any more," I said. I looked back at Lynn. "Do you have a credit card?"

"He'd know," she said softly.

"Not 'til he gets the bill," I said.

"When I don't come back..."

"He'll find her," Matt said.

"Then let's have it out now. I'll go to the house with you while you pack some things, and we'll take along a witness. I can get the divorce suit filed and the preliminary injunction in place this afternoon."

Matt looked at his mother hopefully.

"You can do this," I said, though I myself had never been married and didn't know what I was talking about. "You need to do this."

Lynn stood. "I'll think about it," she said. "I'll think about it and let you know."

Matt stayed in his seat, looking as if he were in pain.

"Take a picture of your face before it heals," I said. "A close up. Keep it in a safe place, and let me know when you make up your mind. If anything else happens, call me."

"It's Matt," Lynn said. "At this point in his life he doesn't need..."

"An abusive father," Matt interrupted. "Nobody does. Don't use me as an excuse for letting this go. I don't have to live at home, anyway, with him or with you. I can move into an apartment."

"You're about to get married," his mother said.

"Exactly," he said, getting up to face her. "I can move in with Melissa."

"No. I don't want you to rush that."

"I can do it. It won't be like you and Dad." He looked down at me. "Mom married in haste," he said. "It was my fault."

"It wasn't your fault," his mother protested. "You weren't even born."

"I was *in utero*," Matt told me. His mother sank back into her chair, looking stricken. "The wedding was in early February," Matt said. "I was born August 30."

I did the mental arithmetic. "Two months premature?"

"I weighed nine-and-a-half pounds. Some preemie, huh?"

"How long have you…" Lynn trailed off.

"Dad's never liked me. Why would he? I'm the matchmaker who put together his happy home. It's like I held the shotgun."

"When…" She got the word out and seemed to run out of air.

"I figured it out when I was fifteen." His shoulders tensed. He took a breath, then said, "A few weeks ago, I started wondering about something else."

His mother looked at him, but it was clear she wasn't going to ask.

"I've begun to wonder if I'm even his. I don't look like him. He's square-headed and barrel-bodied and has that reddish complexion. I'm…" He gestured at his face. I nodded. Both of us looked at Lynn.

She said, "I don't want to talk about this."

"That's not an answer, Mom."

"I don't want to talk about it." She looked at me. "Thank you for your time, Ms. Starling."

"Robin," I said. "Sorry about these…" My eyes cut to Matt. "…complications. But you think about what I've told you. You don't have to live with an abuser." I scribbled my home phone number on the back of one of my business cards and walked around the desk to give it to her. "If anything else happens, anything at all, you call me."

Chapter 2

That evening, I was in the middle of my five-mile run, when Brooke, my roommate, drew up beside me in her car. The door swung open, and I looked into the interior.

"Get in," Brooke said.

I thought at once that someone in my family had died. I got in. "What is it?" I asked, sitting forward to keep my sweaty back off Brooke's seat.

"One of your clients called, a Lynn Nolan." Brooke had the car moving, doing a tight U-turn in the middle of the street.

I felt a wash of relief at the assurance that I wasn't suddenly an orphan or an only child.

"Something's happened, and they need you right away."

"What's happened?" I said.

"She didn't say, but she sounded urgent. She wanted to know how long it would take you to get there. I told her fifteen minutes."

"I've got to take a shower."

"There isn't time."

"I'm sweating like a..."

"I know. You stink, but she really sounded panicky. You've got to go." She reached into the backseat, pulled forward a pair of jeans and a cotton top, and dropped them onto my bare, slick legs. I lifted them quickly in an effort to keep them dry, though my hands were as sweaty as the rest of me.

Brooke turned into the alley that ran behind our house and triggered the garage door remote. "I told her you were on your way."

I rolled my eyes, opened the car door, and stepped out into the driveway. "I hate emergencies," I said. I shucked out of my exercise bra and into the shirt Brooke had brought me. "You might have brought along some underwear."

"I didn't think of it. She—"

"…was panicky. I know." I pushed down my running shorts and stepped out of them. The run had raised my body temperature enough that the crisp October air felt good on my bare skin. I pulled on my jeans.

"Oh. Here are your wallet and keys." She reached across the seat with them.

"Thanks. Drive on into the garage so I can get my car out." I slammed the car door.

Just east of downtown Richmond, the cross streets off Main Street rose steeply. I turned my Volkswagen Beetle onto one of them. The brick homes on either side were occupied, but unlighted for the most part, no more than tall, rectangular shadows against the pale night sky. I turned again onto Grace Street, back in the direction of downtown. After a block and a half, I pulled over against the curb and parked. I tucked my wallet under the seat, got out and beeped the lock. The evening had gotten colder, and I had no jacket.

I was in historic Church Hill, Richmond's earliest community. A couple of blocks further on, Grace Street ends in a overlook of downtown Richmond which at night is spectacular enough to give a girl high, romantic feelings when a guy has his hand inside her shirt. Don't ask me how I know.

At the house I wanted, stairs went up and down from the brick sidewalk: up to the formal rooms of the house, down to what used to be the servants' quarters. There was a bulldog tied to the wrought-iron railing. The bulldog didn't seem belligerent, but I kept my eyes on it as I went up the steps to the wide double doors. The bulldog's head didn't move, though its eyes followed me incuriously.

At the top, I saw that the right-hand door was standing open a few inches, but I knocked anyway. Matt Nolan appeared in the entrance hall.

"Hi, Ms. Starling," he said. "Thanks for coming."

I nodded, watching his eyes cut to my unsupported breasts. "Sure," I said, wishing I had taken a minute to run back inside the house for a clean bra.

"We're all in here."

He led the way to the living room, where a redhead in her mid-twenties sat on the couch. Several people stood around her. She was clearly the center of attention, not entirely because her short skirt had ridden up to the tops of her thighs, though that probably helped, at least with Matt Nolan and the forty-something-year-old man who stood looking down at her.

Lynn Nolan said to the man, "This is Robin Starling, our attorney." Her black eye had darkened, and her blonde hair shone like silk in the living room lighting, softer than the harsh fluorescents of my office building.

"What's going on?" I asked, conscious of the sweaty dampness of my own hair, pulled back into an unflattering ponytail.

"I was attacked," the girl on the couch said.

"Not sexually," Lynn said quickly.

The girl on the couch eyed her. "Someone hit me in the head as he ran up the steps out front. They're saying it was Mr. Nolan."

"This was on the steps right outside the front door?" I asked.

"The steps coming up from the basement to the sidewalk."

"Where is Mr. Nolan now?"

Nobody seemed to know.

"Did somebody call the police? Even if we can't get them to do anything, we need to make this a matter of public record." To the middle-aged man who was keeping a solicitous eye on the visible patch of the redhead's panties, I said, "Where do you come in?"

He started. "She was unconscious," he said. "I found her lying on the steps out there. Actually, Rex found her. She was below the level of the sidewalk, so I might not have seen her. Rex is my dog. I'm Charles Rogers."

He wore a light jacket against the October chill, and his thick, dark hair had a windblown look.

"You said to call you if anything else happened," Lynn said.

I nodded. "And who is…" I jerked my head at the redhead on the couch.

"Melissa Butler," Lynn said. "Matt's fiancée."

"Has Derek ever been violent toward her before?"

"He'd never even met her."

"I didn't know she was here," Matt said. "It might have been hours before we found her if it hadn't been for Mr. Rogers. A friend dropped her off."

I glanced in Mr. Rogers' direction and caught him staring at my chest. It amazes me sometimes that men ever came to assume dominant positions in society, given their easy distractibility.

Melissa Butler said, "I think I hit my head on the steps when I fell. I don't really remember."

"Then how do you…"

"This man came charging out the door, stopped dead at the sight of me, and that's the last thing I knew before Matt was bending over me, and my head was throbbing." She reached out and took Matt's hand. He squeezed her hand, and they smiled at each other.

"I didn't touch her," Mr. Rogers said. "I came up to the house."

"But it was Derek Nolan you saw downstairs," I said to Melissa. "You recognized him."

She shook her head and winced. "I've never met him."

"That's right. Would you know the man if you saw him again?"

"Sure. I think so."

I looked at Mrs. Nolan. "It's time to call the police. We need to get a record of this."

"What do I tell them?"

"Just tell them what happened. Your husband clubbed your son's fiancée to the ground and ran off. While they're here, you can show them your eye." There was a cordless phone sitting on the coffee table. Setting down my keys beside it, I picked it up and punched in 9-1-1. I handed Lynn the phone.

She punched it off. "I can't."

"Why can't you?"

"He'll kill me." She put the phone down, almost as if she were afraid to have it in her possession.

"Derek?"

"Yes. The best thing for me to do is..." She trailed off.

"What?" I said.

"Just not be here when he gets back."

The phone rang. Lynn started to reach for it.

"Wait," I said. "If that's 9-1-1 calling back, and you tell them there's nothing wrong, it's going to be harder for us to tell a different story later."

The phone kept ringing. On the third ring, Charles Rogers, who after all was only a neighbor, said, "Maybe I'd better go. I live just over on Franklin Street if you need me. I'm in the phone book."

Matt shook his hand by way of thanks, and Rogers left. The phone stopped ringing, and in the silence that followed we could hear him talking to his dog in a gooey voice: "Good boy, Rex. Good boy. You're quite the detective, aren't you?"

"So you think you can leave your husband now?" I asked. "You'll go to a hotel?"

"Yes."

I looked at Melissa. "How does it happen you'd never met your fiancé's father?"

"I don't know. I just hadn't."

"We only got engaged a couple of days ago," Matt said.

"And she was going by herself to meet him," I said.

We all looked at Melissa.

"I hadn't planned on it," she said. "I was coming to see Matt, and when I saw a light on down there, I thought I'd introduce myself."

"As Matt's fiancée?"

"As a friend of his. Then it would be easier to break the big news later."

"How long ago was this? Time enough for Derek to have come back?"

They exchanged glances, but no one said anything.

"Let's go look," I said.

"Don't you think we'd better...?" Lynn trailed off.

"Wait for the police?" I smiled humorlessly.

Matt, too, seemed disinclined to take the lead in going down to the basement apartment, so I took the lead myself. They followed. When I stopped to pull the front door open the rest of the way, Lynn was so close behind me that I almost hit her with it. Behind her, Melissa and Matt were holding hands.

We went out onto the porch and down the steps. The sidewalk was deserted. The occasional car was parked along the curb, mine closest to the house. Charles Rogers and his dog had disappeared into the shadows.

"Is that yours?" Melissa asked, and I glanced at her.

"The Beetle? Yeah, it's mine."

"I've always liked those."

"Me, too. Lots of headroom for a little car." I wondered whether she was a space cadet or merely trying to be friendly. Leaving the sidewalk, I went down the steps to a single, solid door. There was a copper lamp fixed onto the brick beside the door, lighting the steps well enough that Charles Rogers might have noticed a short-skirted woman lying on them, even without the help of Rex the canine detective. On the door itself was a brass plaque that carried the name Derek Nolan and, below it, the single word "Factor." The door was locked. There was no window, illuminated or otherwise.

"I'll get the key," Matt said, and disappeared back up the steps.

"What's a factor?" I asked Lynn.

"A money lender."

"A loan shark," Melissa said. She flushed when Lynn looked at her. "That's what Matt calls him."

"Specifically, it's someone who lends money to businesses," Lynn said. "Manufacturers and dealers."

"He can compete with the banks?"

"Sometimes he's willing to make loans a bank wouldn't."

"Ah," I said.

Matt came back with his mother's purse. "The key by the door's gone," he said as he handed the purse to her.

"Did you forget to put it back?"

"I never use it. No one does, except in emergencies."

Frowning irritably, Lynn fished out a set of keys, sorted through it one-handed, and gave me the set with the appropriate key extended.

I twisted the key in the lock and depressed the latch.

The apartment was as dark as a cave. I felt for a switch and found it. A floor lamp with a Tiffany shade came on, revealing a well-appointed office, though the chair behind the large walnut desk had been overturned. Stepping forward, I saw that a man was on the floor by the chair, lying on his back with one arm out-flung. His face seemed distorted, his ear dark with blood that ran down from his temple to an irregular stain on the Oriental carpet.

Behind me someone gasped. I think it was Lynn, but when I looked back all three of them seemed to have retreated into the doorway beside a smaller desk, which was set at a right angle to the front wall. My own heart was hammering, and when I spoke, my voice seemed to have a hollow quality. "Derek?" I asked.

Lynn nodded. She had a knuckle pressed to her mouth, and the skin around her unblemished eye looked slightly pink.

"Is this the man who hit you?" I asked Melissa.

She shrugged, wide-eyed.

"When you say you saw a light on down here, did you mean the outside light?"

She was looking at me like a deer caught in the headlights.

"Or did you see a line of light under the door or something?"

"I don't know," she said.

"You don't know?"

"I don't remember." She turned away from me and pushed through the door.

"You don't need to cross-examine her," Matt said, before going after her.

I looked at Lynn and shrugged. "Occupational hazard," I said by way of apology. I took a step back toward the door and saw Matt and Melissa sitting together on the steps. He had his arm around her.

I turned and walked back to the desk to look over things more carefully. Though I had practiced law for only six years and criminal law was not my specialty, I was a lawyer at a crime scene with her client. I could feel the weight of responsibility.

One of the file drawers in the desk was open. It was fitted with hanging folders and was crammed to capacity. Lynn, beside me, asked, "What do you think happened?"

"I think somebody shot him in the side of the head," I said. It was a crass way to put it, but it didn't seem to faze her. She moved around me and stood looking down at her dead husband.

"Why would anybody do that?"

I didn't respond.

"It could have been suicide," she said in a hopeful tone.

"No gun," I said. There was something clutched in the man's out-flung fist, but it wasn't that.

"He has one in his desk."

"Who put it back for him?"

She looked confused. "What?"

"If Derek had killed himself, the gun would be there on the floor beside him."

"Unless someone moved it afterwards."

"Who?"

"The man who knocked Melissa down?" But her voice was uncertain.

15

"If he found the body, what motive would he have for making it look like murder?"

Lynn took an awkward step sideways, her eyes fixed on her dead husband. I thought for a moment she was going to fall.

"We need to back out of here," I said, taking her arm. "We've got to call the police, and it would be better not to use the phone on the desk."

Lynn nodded. "I know. I just can't..." She bumped against the credenza. A file folder fell to the floor, spilling papers, and a computer screen came on. "I can't..."

"You just put your left hand on the credenza," I said. "Let's try not to touch anything else." A Word document had appeared on the screen. It looked like a promissory note made for the signature of someone named Turk.

Seeing my focus, Lynn turned to look, too. Her attention shifted to the printer. She picked up the single page before I could stop her.

"Look at this," she said, and she turned the page so I could read the printing: *Matt, Lynn, I'm sorry. I haven't been much of a husband or a father. I've become something I never intended to be. I'm sick of myself and everything around me.*

There was no signature, not even a typed one.

After a moment, Lynn said, "A suicide note."

"Still no gun," I said. "And anybody could have typed this. It would be nice if your fingerprints weren't on it."

She put the paper back on the printer just as a new voice sounded from the steps outside. "Is everybody all right here?"

Matt said something in response, but I couldn't make out the words. I went around the desk to the door. A uniformed police officer was on the steps with Matt, his partner standing above him at the top of the stairs.

"We've got a body down here," I said.

"A body." He didn't look as if he believed me, but he gestured to his partner. "What kind of body?"

"A dead one." I stepped aside to let them past me into the apartment. "Where's Melissa?" I asked Matt.

"In the house. She was feeling kind of sick."

I nodded. "How about you? You all right?"

"I'm fine," he said. He smiled at me, but he looked grim. I turned back into the apartment, and Matt came after me. Already one of the cops was on his cell phone, and the other stood over the body.

The crime scene had changed. Dread settled over me as I walked closer, noting the differences. The promissory note no longer showed on the computer screen, only a picture of Lynn and Matt and a few icons along the left side. The file drawer in the desk was now closed. More significantly, a small automatic pistol lay on the carpet by the dead man's left shoulder, just outside the bloodstain. My eyes went to Lynn's face, and she looked back defiantly.

A wave of anger surged through me.

The cop flipped his cell phone closed. "Who are you people?" he asked me.

"Robin Starling."

"Lynn Nolan. I live here. This is my husband."

"I'm Matt Nolan," Matt said.

"You live here too?"

He said he did.

"You?" the cop asked me.

I shook my head. "I just got here. I'm a lawyer."

The cop's eyes went to Lynn. "How come you called a lawyer?"

I said, "I was talking to her about a divorce. We didn't know her husband was down here until about three minutes ago."

"Huh. Look, we're going to ask all of you to wait outside until homicide gets here." He locked eyes with his partner and jerked his head in our direction.

"Come on. Let's go," the partner said to us.

"May we wait upstairs in the house?" Lynn asked.

"Sure. Upstairs is fine."

My red Beetle was pulling away from the curb as we went out. I took the remaining steps two at a time, but I was too late. By the time I reached the street, my car was turning the corner half a block away.

"What the hell," I said as I came to a stop.

Matt Nolan was looking at me as if I'd gone berserk on him. "What is it?" he said.

"That was my car."

"Your car. Who was driving it?"

"Your girlfriend, I think. I left my keys on the coffee table upstairs."

"Melissa." He was sprinting up the steps into the main part of the house as his mother reached the sidewalk. Both cops were still down in Derek's office.

Lynn and I went up the stairs toward the door of the house, which Matt had left open. "I hope you know what you're doing," I said to Lynn as the front door closed behind us, leaving us alone in the front hall. "What you tell me is privileged communication.

What I see is something else again. I can be made to testify about that."

"It has to look like suicide," she insisted.

"Unless the gun in the desk is the gun that fired the fatal bullet, it's not going to look like a suicide."

"If the scene's convincing enough..."

"Had the desk gun been fired recently? It's an automatic. Is there an ejected casing somewhere in that office?"

She looked dismayed.

"Why did you close the document that was open on the computer?"

"Because it doesn't make any sense. Why would Derek start work on another document after typing a suicide note?"

"Why would a murderer print the suicide note, then open another file?" I said. "It's not up to us to manufacture evidence that makes sense. We have to deal with the facts as they exist."

"Do you think the murderer brought the suicide note with him?"

"If so, you've done your best to keep the police from considering the possibility. They're going to assume it was composed and printed right here." A thought occurred to me. "You're not covering up for someone, are you?"

"What do you mean?"

"Your husband's dead, and you seem to have surprisingly little interest in what happened to him."

"I don't care what happened to him," she said bitterly. "He's dead, and I just want everything resolved as soon as possible."

"You may not have helped your cause any."

"I guess we'll see, won't we?"

"I guess we will."

Matt was coming down the stairs from the floor above. "She's gone," he said.

"Gone? Who's gone?" Lynn asked.

"Melissa. She's gone."

"Evidently, she just drove away in my car," I said.

"Why would she do that?"

"How should I know? She's your son's fiancée."

"I just met her a couple of days ago myself," Lynn said. "After they became engaged."

I looked at Matt. "You were dating her secretly?"

"Not exactly. I just haven't brought her around the house much."

"Where'd you meet her?"

"At a coffee shop up by VCU. She's a waitress."

"VCU where you go to school?" A siren was audible on the night air and growing louder.

Matt nodded.

"Where does Melissa live?"

"She has an apartment in the Fan, not far from the university. Why?"

"Just trying to get a handle on where she might have taken my car."

"Yeah, I guess you're kind of stuck, aren't you?"

"Yes, I am, and under the circumstances, I'd like to get out of here before the police can ask me too many questions." I wondered suddenly if Melissa might have had the same motivation.

"What circumstances?" Matt asked.

"Ask your mother."

Chapter 3

I called my roommate Brooke to come get me. Before she got there, though, a homicide detective I knew came in the front door and stopped in the archway to the living room.

"Robin Starling," he said, sounding surprised.

I looked up. "Hi, Jordan."

"Not a good sign," he said. "Murder cases becoming your specialty?"

"Let's hope not." It was, I reflected, the second murder scene at which he'd found me.

Lynn said, "This wasn't murder, though. It was suicide, wasn't it?"

"Doubtful," Jordan said.

"Why do you say that?" I asked.

The corner of Jordan's mouth lifted. "It's what I always say."

"So you don't have any specific reasons for thinking it wasn't suicide?"

"That's not what I said." He came into the living room and sat in a large square chair, pushing the ottoman out of the way with his foot. "Tell me about it," he said, his eyes on Lynn Nolan.

"About finding the body?"

"That will do for starters."

She told him, starting with Charles Rogers ringing the doorbell and about finding Melissa Butler on the steps outside. Jordan wrote the names in his notebook, but seemed to be relying on his memory for the rest of it.

"So she saw a man fleeing the scene," he said. "Did she describe him?"

"Well, no," Lynn said. "Not really. We all just assumed it was Derek."

"Derek is your husband?"

She nodded.

"And that's whose body is downstairs."

Again the quick nod. "Derek has a history of violence," Lynn said. "And he's been in a bad mood lately."

"He do that to your eye?"

Lynn nodded.

"Where is Melissa Butler? I'd like to talk to her."

They all looked at me, and Jordan's eyes followed their gaze.

"She's driving around in my car," I said.

"Just driving around, or is she going somewhere?"

"I don't know."

"Look. This woman saw the murderer. You can't just bury her."

"I didn't bury her."

"But you sent her off in your car."

"No, I didn't."

He shifted in the chair. "You see, the problem is I know you, Robin. You do whatever the hell you want, and you depend on constant motion to stay out of trouble."

"Well, I didn't send her off in my car. I left my keys in the house when we went downstairs. We discovered the body, then the police came. When they shooed us out of the downstairs apartment, my car was pulling away from the curb."

"With Ms. Butler at the wheel."

"I assume so. I didn't actually see her. She was up in the house, though, and my keys are missing."

"Along with Ms. Butler herself."

I didn't say anything.

"I want to talk to her," Jordan said. He looked at Lynn, then Matt, then me.

"Join the club," I said.

"Why was she up in the house anyway? Was she alone?"

"She was alone. Finding the body seemed to upset her."

"And after the police came, she left with your car."

I shrugged, then nodded.

"Without your knowledge or permission."

"Without my permission. I knew about it, because I saw her doing it."

"No particular reason you want to keep her from talking to the police," Jordan said.

"Of course not."

"So you want to report your car stolen?"

I shook my head.

His mouth stretched. "I thought not."

"I don't want to prosecute, at least not until I hear what she has to say for herself. I don't have any objection to you putting out an APB or whatever it is and having the car picked up."

"Okay, then." Jordan looked at Matt. "Can you give me her address?"

Matt moved his head, but looked unwilling.

"For heaven's sake," Jordan said. "I just want to talk to her."

"Okay, okay. She lives in an apartment building on Franklin Street. 1313 Franklin, apartment B."

Jordan got up and left the house, leaving the front door open. Lynn and Matt and I looked at each other. "You don't have any idea why she ran off?" I asked. "Either of you?"

"I haven't a clue," Lynn said. Matt shook his head, looking unhappy.

"Could she have killed Derek and fallen on the steps on the way out?"

"She didn't know Dad. Why would she kill him?"

Lynn said, "The door was locked, and she didn't have a key."

A cold draft from the open door swept across me, and I shivered. "Didn't Matt say the key by the door was missing? It's why he brought you your purse." If Melissa had had a key, I thought, she now had the time and the whole city of Richmond in which to dispose of it.

Jordan came back in, pushing the door shut behind him. He went back to his chair and sat down again. "Okay," he said to Lynn. "Go on with your story."

"There's not much left to tell. We went downstairs and found the body."

"Before or after you dialed 9-1-1?"

Lynn's gaze started to slide toward me, but she stopped it. "After," she said.

"What made you think your husband had knocked down Ms. Butler?"

"I don't know. She said it was a man coming out of the downstairs apartment. I didn't know who else would be down there."

Matt said, "He's a violent man. It wouldn't have been the first time."

"He's knocked Ms. Butler down before?"

Lynn said, "No, he didn't mean that."

"I mean look at Mom's eye," Matt said.

They were giving themselves a motive for killing Derek, and I wondered whether I should be letting them talk.

"What did she say about this man on the steps, other than he knocked her down?"

Matt shrugged. Lynn said, "Nothing."

"Was he tall or short, thin or stocky..."

"She didn't say."

"And you didn't ask her."

"No."

"Dark hair, facial hair? Any description at all that made this man sound like he could be Derek Nolan?"

She shook her head, and Jordan looked at Matt. He shook his head, too. Jordan sighed.

"Back to your discovery of the body," he said. "You went downstairs, then what?"

"Ms. Starling unlocked the door and opened it. The apartment was dark. When she flipped the light switch, there didn't seem to be a desk chair behind my husband's desk. We didn't see the body at first."

I opened my mouth to describe the crime scene as we actually found it, thinking a prompt admission and apology would serve better in the long run than a lie. Before I could say a word, though, the doorbell rang.

I exhaled through my open mouth.

Matt said, "I'll get it." From the entrance hall, he said, "It's Melissa," and he flung open the door.

"Oh," he said.

It was my roommate. "I'm Brooke Marshall. Is Robin Starling here?"

"In here, Brooke," I called.

Brooke came in, and I realized that she did resemble Melissa Butler. They were about the same height and weight and had the same red hair, though Brooke was several years older and their complexions were different, Brooke's peaches-and-cream, Melissa's freckled and her face narrower. Still, the resemblance was remarkable.

Matt followed Brooke in, and Jordan stood. "Ms. Butler?"

I shook my head. "You remember Brooke Marshall," I said. "She's my ride home."

"Oh," he said. "So you weren't the one who got knocked down on the steps outside?"

"Sorry to disappoint."

Jordan looked at Matt. "They look a lot alike?"

"I guess not," he said, his eyes on Brooke. "Not really."

"How long have you known Melissa Butler?" Jordan asked him.

"Six months."

"And you've been engaged how long?"

"A week."

"You say she's a student?"

"No, I'm a student at VCU. Melissa works at O'Riley's."

Jordan nodded. To me he said, "Your ride's here. Are you leaving?"

"I'd better stay until you finish questioning my clients."

"You can sit over here," Matt said to Brooke, gesturing her to the sofa. She gave him a smile and he sat down next to her. Matt was a hound dog, I thought.

Jordan said to Lynn, "You were just telling us about finding your husband."

"Yes," she said. "We couldn't see him from the doorway, but as we walked forward we could see him lying on his back in the overturned chair, his left arm against his body, his right arm almost straight out."

I started to speak, but Jordan cut me off. "Was your husband right-handed or left-handed?"

Lynn said, "Right handed."

"You saw the gun next to his right shoulder?"

"Yes."

I exhaled. The lie was told, and I had let it happen.

"But something else was in his right hand," Jordan said.

Her eyes shifted, but she didn't say anything.

"What was in his right hand?" I asked.

"A cell phone," Jordan said.

"Are you thinking he was trying to call someone?"

"I don't know."

"Was it Derek's iPhone?" Lynn asked.

"I don't know. Did he have an iPhone?"

Lynn nodded.

"Did any of you touch anything?"

Lynn shook her head, but I said, "Lynn read the sheet of paper on the printer and put it back."

There was a flash of anger in Lynn's eyes as she turned her gaze toward me, but I ignored it.

"Her prints are probably on the paper," I said. "I think it was the note that made her think of suicide."

"That and the gun," she said. It made me want to choke her.

"The gun by his right shoulder," Jordan said.

"Yes."

"And of course he was shot in the right side of the head."

"He shot himself."

"That's right. You said he was right-handed, didn't you?"

"Yes."

"Do you think he picked up the cell phone in his right hand before or after firing the shot?"

Lynn's face became still.

"It would have been awkward for him to fire that shot with his left hand," Jordan said. "I'm not sure he could have done it. It would have been just as awkward to fire the shot while holding the gun and cell phone together in the same hand—and remarkable that he maintained his grip on the cell phone, but not the gun, when he went over backwards in the chair."

"That's why you don't think it was suicide?" I asked.

Jordan's eyes left Lynn's face unwillingly, and he looked at me. "That's enough for starters."

"Anyway," Lynn said. "We were standing and looking down at the body when the police showed up."

"Not quite," Jordan reminded her.

"What?"

"You picked that paper off the printer, looked at it, and put it back down."

"Well, yes," she conceded.

"What else did you touch?"

She shook her head. "Nothing."

"The desk?"

"I may have placed a palm on it when I saw Derek lying there. I don't know."

"Touch anything on the desk?"

"No."

"The computer? Something on the credenza? Anything at all?"

She shook her head.

"Ms. Starling?" His gaze shifted to me.

"I didn't touch anything," I said.

"Did you see Ms. Nolan or anyone else touch anything other than the paper on the printer and the surface of the desk?"

Here it was, and, unfortunately, the way he had asked the question made it possible for me to be dishonest without actually lying. "No," I said. "I didn't see anybody touch anything else." All of it had happened while my back was turned.

Chapter 4

Eventually, the Nolans, Lynn and Matt, went upstairs to pack, and I left with Brooke. The Nolans were going to the Berkeley Hotel, which was in nearby Shockoe Slip, an old but upscale commercial district on the near edge of downtown Richmond. At least for this one night, the police wanted sole possession of the house.

Brooke rolled through the tollbooth on the Downtown Expressway, and I continued my account of finding the body and of the tampering Lynn Nolan had done with the crime scene: pushing in a drawer, closing a document on the computer, getting a gun from the desk and dropping it by the body.

"Why would she do that?" Brooke said.

I was silent, my eyes on the big green sign that announced the upcoming junction with I-64. "I don't know," I said at last.

"Don't you think—"

"Get off here," I said. "Let's go back."

Brooke steered the car onto the exit ramp. "What do you have in mind?" she asked.

"I'm not sure. I'm afraid for Lynn suddenly. The police aren't as dumb as she thinks they are."

Brooke crossed over the Expressway and got back on it, heading back into downtown Richmond. "What I don't get is why you didn't tell the police about her tampering with the evidence," she said.

"She's my client."

"But you're a witness."

"I know. What I saw isn't protected by client confidentiality."

"So…"

I shook my head. "I don't know. Client loyalty, I guess. I'm not going to be called as a witness against my own client, not if I can help it."

She exited onto Byrd Street and, as the pavement dropped away from us, took her foot off the accelerator. Byrd Street was steep, and Brooke had to use the brake to control our speed. "Do you think they're at the hotel yet?"

"If not, we can wait for them in the lobby."

When we got to the hotel, Brooke turned the corner, and the car vibrated over cobblestones. Shockoe Slip had been a warehouse district before the Civil War. On a Friday night, parking was at a premium, but just past The Tobacco Company, a bar and restaurant housed in one of the renovated warehouses, a car was pulling away from the curb.

Brooke slid into the open spot. "That was lucky," she said.

"Maybe it's an omen."

A gust of rain came out of nowhere and spattered the windshield.

"Maybe that's our omen," Brooke said.

"Let's hope not." I pushed open the door of the car and got out. Another spatter of rain caught me in the face. I could see a curtain of rain sweeping up the cobblestones toward us.

"Come on," I said. "Let's hurry."

"I can feel my hair frizzing," Brooke said, her hands in her pockets and her shoulders hunched. The sky was spitting droplets at us.

My own hair was a straight, shiny blonde. "I should be so lucky," I said.

"What are you talking about? You have great hair," Brooke said.

The rain swept past us as we reached the canopy that overhung the steps of the hotel, and we stood for a moment watching it on the shining cobblestones as it drummed the canopy above our heads. Brooke glanced at me, and I shrugged. We turned and went up into the Berkeley. The dining room off the lobby was closed. I glanced at my watch and saw that it was just after eleven.

There were two clerks at the registration desk, a geeky white guy with a pale, thin face and a light-skinned black woman who could have been a model. Neither was over twenty-five. "Welcome to the Berkeley," the woman said brightly.

"Hi," I said. "A Lynn and Matt Nolan are supposed to be checking in tonight. Could you tell me if they're here yet?"

The woman tapped something into a keyboard, glanced at the screen, and said, "Yes. They checked in a few minutes ago."

"Could you ring them for me?" I knew better than to ask for room numbers.

"Which? Lynn or Matt?"

"Lynn," I said.

She picked up the phone and tapped in a number. After a quarter-minute she moved the receiver away from her ear. "No answer," she said.

"Matt, then."

"Okay." He was there. "Hello, Mr. Nolan, this is registration. There's someone in the lobby asking to speak with you." She looked at me.

"Robin Starling," I said.

She repeated it, nodded, then gestured to a phone on the wall to one side of the registration desk. "You can use that phone," she said to me.

I went and picked it up.

"Ms. Starling?"

"Hi, Matt," I said. "Sorry to disturb you. Is your mother there?"

"She has her own room two down from me. Three twenty-one."

"She doesn't answer."

Matt was silent.

"Any idea where she might be?"

"No," he said. I found that I didn't believe him, though I couldn't imagine why he would lie.

I sighed into the phone. "I guess it's not important," I said. "I'll just talk to her in the morning." I hung up the phone, nodded my thanks to the woman at the registration desk, then went into a brief huddle with Brooke.

"You wait here," I said. "If Lynn Nolan or Matt Nolan leaves the hotel, follow them."

"Okay, but…"

I couldn't stay to hear the rest of it. I headed for the elevators, nodding matter-of-factly to the woman at the desk. She didn't challenge me. Rather than wait for an elevator, I pushed through the fire door into the stairwell and took the steps two at a time. When I got to the third floor, the elevator doors were closing on someone, but I was too late to see whom. There was a man in the hall standing in the doorway of his room. He was wearing Dockers, a white shirt, and a striped tie. To me he looked like a cop, but maybe I was just being paranoid.

Back in the stairwell, I raced back down to the first floor, jumping the last half-dozen steps in each set of stairs, grabbing the rail to make the turn at each landing. I went out into the hall and looked at the lights above the elevator I'd seen leaving three. It was on the fourth floor. I went back through the fire door.

Though I'm in good shape, I was blowing hard by the time I reached the fourth floor. I was just in time to see Matt going into a room at the far end of the hall. Half-running, half-walking, I tried to keep my eyes on the spot where he had disappeared.

He had gone into either room 437 or room 439. As I stood between them, shifting from one foot to the other, I heard ice hitting a bucket at the end of the hall. I knocked on the door of room 439, then went to the door of room 437 and knocked on it, too.

The door of 437 was the first to open. The man who opened it was slightly taller than I was. His shaved head and flat belly gave him an athletic appearance, though he was probably in his forties. I glanced at 439 and beyond it to where a woman wearing black jeans and a polo shirt was coming out of the ice room with her bucket. I pushed past the man into his room, ignoring his exclamation of protest.

"Close the door," I said, but it wasn't necessary. As he turned, he let go of the door and it swung shut behind him. The door to the bathroom was shut. The beds were made, but both had been sat on. I went past the beds and took the chair at the desk.

"Who are you?" the man asked me. Beneath dark eyebrows, light glinted from narrow, black-framed glasses.

"I'm Robin Starling," I said in a loud voice.

"So? What do you want?"

I waited. The door to the bathroom opened, and Lynn came out.

"Hello, Mrs. Nolan," I said.

"What are you doing here?" Her voice was angry, but her eyes were a little too wide to go with the voice. She looked frightened.

Matt came out behind her.

"Quite the party," I said. "Are you going to introduce me?"

Lynn's eyes went to the man who had opened the door. He shrugged, almost imperceptibly, but she hesitated.

"We may not have much time," I said.

"What do you mean?"

"The police are here. They're keeping tabs on you."

Lynn's hand went to her throat, but Matt said belligerently, "I don't believe it."

"Did you see a woman with an ice bucket when you came up here?" I asked him. "Black jeans, pink polo shirt?"

"She rode up in the elevator with me."

"She's one, and she's not the only one." I looked at Lynn and jerked my head in the direction of the man who had let me in.

"My name is Steve Bruno," he said, not waiting for the introduction. "Who are you?"

I'd already given him my name. I said, "I'm Lynn's attorney. What's your connection to the Nolans?"

"A friend."

"What are you doing here? Why did they come to this hotel to meet you?"

"I don't know that they did."

"I'm sure you know that Derek Nolan was murdered tonight. The police are going to be able to establish that Lynn Nolan came to your room immediately after checking in. Is there any reason that would be undesirable?"

Lynn and Bruno exchanged glances.

"If there's a history between you that's going to interest the police, I need to hear it," I said.

Unexpectedly, Matt spoke up. "Steven Bruno graduated from East High School in Charlotte, North Carolina, the same year as my mother. They both went to the University of Richmond, but Bruno only finished three semesters. In May of the year he dropped out, Mom married an MBA student named Derek Nolan."

Lynn looked shocked, but she shouldn't have been. We already knew Matt had been doing his homework. She said, "How do you know all that?"

"Internet. Information cost me fifty bucks."

"Do you live in Richmond?" I asked Bruno.

"No, though I've been here for the past month."

"Staying at this hotel?" That had to be expensive. "How often have you seen Lynn during that time?"

He didn't say anything.

"He's seen her a lot," Matt said.

His mother said, "Matt, what are you saying?"

Matt looked uncomfortable, but he said, "It's time you get honest with me. I want to know who my father is." It was as if he'd detonated a small bomb. Lynn and Bruno were still standing, but with their insides blown out. Matt's paternity wasn't my immediate concern, though.

"How many times have you seen Derek Nolan?" I asked Bruno.

He shook his head.

"Does that mean you haven't seen him? Are you the one Melissa Butler saw leaving the house on Grace Street tonight?"

"Who is Melissa Butler?"

"My fiancée," Matt said. "You haven't met her."

"She's a redhead," I said. "Somebody knocked her down on the steps coming up from the basement apartment."

Bruno shook his head. "It wasn't me."

"But you have been at the house on Grace Street," I said.

"Who says I have? You don't have any basis for that accusation."

"That's not a denial."

"Who do you think you are, anyway?"

"She's representing us," Lynn said.

"That doesn't explain what she's doing in my room cross-examining me in the middle of the night."

"I'm trying to keep everybody out of jail," I said. "Did you kill Derek Nolan?"

"No. I didn't know he was dead until Lynn told me just now."

I looked at Lynn. "Bruno's not the one you were trying to protect?"

She hesitated.

"Never mind. Did you kill your husband?"

"No."

To Matt I said, "Did you kill your father?"

"I'm not sure Derek is ..."

"Your legal father," I cut in. "I'm not concerned right now with who was sleeping with whom twenty years ago." I realized immediately just how tactless that was, but it was too late to recall the words. "Did you kill him?"

"I didn't kill him," Matt said.

I looked at the three of them. "Do any of you know who did?"

I got one "no" and two headshakes. I wasn't sure I believed them, but it was going to have to do for a working hypothesis.

"Okay," I said. "Then we can stop with the cover-up. Nobody needs to protect anybody, and we can concentrate on finding out what happened." I went to the phone. "Let me set something up and then I have a few more questions." I picked up the phone, glancing at the directions on the face of the instrument, and then dialed nine and the number of Brooke's cell phone. I didn't have my own cell; it was probably somewhere in my bedroom.

Brooke answered on the second ring.

"Are you still in the lobby?" I asked.

"Yes."

"Seen much activity?"

"A little. Some men coming and going."

"They may be cops. Do you think you can leave the hotel without attracting attention? Go out to your car."

"Okay."

"I want you to call the hotel and make a reservation."

"For tonight?"

"For tonight. Ask for room 439. Be talkative. Say you stayed in the room once with a boyfriend and you'd like to stay there again for sentimental reasons."

"So I'm a slut, but a sentimental slut." There was a pause. "Okay, I'm outside. Fortunately, the rain's let up. It's just a drizzle now. What's the number of the hotel?"

I read it off the phone. "For luggage you can get your gym bag out of the back seat. You might want to put your hair in a ponytail or something so you don't look so much like the woman who's been hanging out in the lobby."

"This isn't going to get me in trouble, is it?"

"I hope not."

"Great."

"If I get you in, I'll get you out again. Make the reservation, then check into the hotel and go up to your room."

"Suppose 439 isn't available?"

"Then we're screwed," I said. "Call me…" I hesitated. "No, never mind. If you can get the room, knock on the connecting door when you get there. If you can't, just stay in the car, and I'll call you."

I hung up.

"What was all that about?" Bruno asked me.

"There're cops swarming all over this hotel," I said. "Something tells me it's going to look bad if they catch the two of you together. Derek Nolan is shot in the head, and that night the police find his widow in the hotel room of an old boyfriend. I don't want those facts ever presented to a jury, though there may be nothing we can do about it."

"So what are you doing?"

"Working desperately on a plan to have some of us gone when they close in. I doubt it will work." I went to the connecting door to room 439 and opened it. On the inside door, there was a chrome disk in place of a doorknob, which prevented the door from being opened from this side.

"She's not much at building confidence, is she?" Bruno murmured to Lynn.

I went back to the desk chair and sat, though Lynn and Bruno were still on their feet. "While we wait, maybe you could tell me about any recent conflicts in Derek Nolan's life," I said, looking at Lynn, then Matt, who had taken a seat on one of the beds.

"I don't understand," Lynn said.

"Somebody wanted him dead. If he was a loan shark, maybe that's not so surprising. Tell me about that."

Matt and Lynn exchanged glances. "I don't think 'loan shark' is quite fair," Lynn said.

Matt said, "There's the embezzlement."

"Embezzlement's good," I said. "Tell me about that."

Lynn said, "Evidently, when Derek was out of the office last month, someone came in to pay off his note early."

"Who?"

"I don't know. Derek didn't tell me."

"Who was running the office?"

"An administrative assistant was supposed to be running it, a woman named Liz Lockard. Evidently, though, she was out when a customer came in with his check. A man named Mark Walker was minding the shop."

"Who's he?"

"An errand boy…"

"A thirty-year-old, two-hundred-fifty-pound errand boy," Matt cut in. "Dad sent him around sometimes to collect payment."

"Mark Walker was there, and Liz wasn't," Lynn said. "Evidently, Walker accepted the check and gave the customer his note back. Then he forged Derek's name to the check and cashed it."

"Seems like a good way to get caught," I said.

"But not immediately. Derek prints out the notes from his computer, and so they're all right there on the hard drive. All Walker had to do was print another copy of the note, forge the customer's signature, and put it back in the file. That bought him some time."

"Time to do what? Did he have a plan to pay the money back before the embezzlement was discovered?"

"We don't know," Lynn said.

Matt said, "I saw him at Colonial Downs once."

Lynn looked at him sharply.

"Melissa likes horses," he said defensively.

"If you were with Melissa, it must have been fairly recently," I said. "Was Walker gambling?"

"I don't know. He was with Liz Lockard, though."

"The office manager," Lynn reminded me.

"What does this Mark Walker look like?"

"He's a big, beefy guy with a bushy horseshoe of hair around his head."

"Muscular?"

She shrugged. "I don't know. I'm sure he's as strong as a horse."

"I don't guess Melissa said anything about the size of the man who knocked her down tonight," I said.

Matt's eyebrows went up. Lynn shook her head. "No. She just said 'a man.'"

I exhaled. "I sure hope the police can pick her up. We badly need to ask her some questions."

"Why would she steal a car and drive away like that?" Lynn asked, sounding querulous.

Matt said, "She didn't steal a car, Mom. She just..."

"Don't say it," his mother said. "Don't say she borrowed it. She took the keys without asking and drove away with it. She'd only just met the owner."

Matt opened his mouth to respond, but I cut him off.

"Back to this embezzlement," I said. "How did Derek find out about it, and what did he do?"

Matt said, "He ran into the debtor at the Commonwealth Club. The guy made some kind of off-hand remark that got them to talking about him paying off the loan, then later he faxed Dad a copy of the note Mark Walker had returned to him. It was stamped 'Paid' and signed by Mark Walker."

"The amount was sixteen thousand dollars or so," Lynn said. "Derek confronted Mark with what he had done, and Mark said he'd make it up to him."

"You mean pay him back?"

"I guess so."

"Derek wasn't going to prosecute?"

"I think he was still hoping to get his money back. This was just a couple of weeks ago. Derek fired him, of course, and once he had his money, he was still likely to prosecute, no matter what he said."

"I think Mark Walker is worth talking to," I said. "Liz Lockard, too."

The door from the next room opened, and we all started. It was Brooke, though, who stuck her head in. "Mission accomplished," she said.

I stood, feeling almost light-headed with relief. "Okay," I said. "Bruno, you stay here in this room. The rest of us will go next door. Actually, they'll go. I'll stay with you."

"What do we do over there?" Lynn asked.

"Spend the night, I think. If you try to leave, somebody's going to see you." I looked at Bruno. "Tell you what. You and I can go across the street to The Tobacco Company. That may force them to revise their theory about what's going on. We can have a couple of drinks, and maybe they'll look in the room while we're gone. If they realize they've missed the Nolans, maybe they'll move their operations elsewhere."

"That's a lot of maybes," Lynn said.

Bruno asked, "Won't they check the next room when they don't find us?"

"I don't know. The room's rented in a stranger's name, and both connecting doors will be closed. Unless you can come up with something else, it's all we've got."

"Let's go," Matt said, giving a tug at his mother's arm.

43

"What about me?" Brooke asked.

"You could leave, I think. You probably ought to. If this doesn't work, there's no point dragging you down with the rest of us."

She shrugged.

"Close the door on your side and lock it," I said. I hurried them through, then closed the door. That left me alone with Bruno, me looking at him, him looking back.

"Do you know what you're doing?" he asked.

"No," I said. "Do you?"

"You've barged in and taken over. I don't know you, and I'm not sure I like it."

"The next few hours should give you a better basis for forming an opinion," I said. "Have you eaten?"

"Hours ago."

"Me, too. I can't say I'm hungry, though. Do you drink?"

"Water."

"Good man. There's a nightclub in the basement of the restaurant across the street. You can buy us a couple of Pellegrinos, and we can listen to some music."

Chapter 5

When we came out of the hotel room, a man was standing in front of the elevators, just punching the call button. As Bruno and I approached him, he glanced incuriously at us and away. The elevator doors slid open, and he got on. The doors stayed open as we approached.

"Thanks," I said as we got on with him.

He took his finger off the button, and the doors slid shut. "You're welcome." He was wearing chinos and a rugby shirt with orange and blue stripes.

"University of Virginia," I said, giving his shirt a nod.

"I'm sorry?"

"UVA colors," I said.

"Oh." He shrugged.

I looked at Bruno and shrugged myself. The doors opened, and we got off on the first floor. Bruno and I went toward the street; the man in the rugby shirt turned toward the desk.

"Is he another one of your policeman?" Bruno asked me as we crossed the cobblestones to the bar.

"Why not?" I said.

We entered the Tobacco Company at the basement level, where music was playing too loudly for easy conversation. Easy chairs and sofas were grouped around low tables on all sides of a small dance floor. No one was dancing, though. Bruno sat down in the center of a love seat. Rather than sit in the chair angled next to it, I squeezed in beside him. He made room for me, though he looked annoyed.

"I want to talk without shouting," I said in a loud voice.

A girl approached to take our drink order. She was as tall as I was, and her short skirt made her legs look so skinny as to be stork-like. I ordered Pellegrino and made a mental note to be careful about very short skirts.

"Scotch and soda," Bruno said.

After the waitress left, I said, "I thought you didn't drink."

His smile was almost a grimace. "I haven't had a drink since I turned thirty."

"Is this the time to start back?" Even though we were sitting right next to each other, we were having to project our voices to be heard over the music.

"I don't know. I'm thinking it might be."

I could understand the impulse. "How come you to leave Lynn all those years ago?" I asked.

"I didn't know she was pregnant."

So Matt was his son. A man came down the steps into the nightclub, walked past us and sat alone in the grouping of chairs just behind us. I leaned into Bruno and said, more softly, "I think we've got company. We're going to have to keep our voices down."

The waitress came with our drinks. Bruno gave her a ten. There wasn't any change. I squeezed the wedge of lime into my water and took a sip. After a quick pull of his own drink, Bruno grinned fiercely and wiped his mouth with the back of his hand. He took another swallow, while I eyed him speculatively.

Finally, Bruno put his arm around me and bent his mouth to my ear. "Is this okay?" he asked.

I nodded. It would have to be.

"I started drinking in college," he said. "The drinking age was 21, but I was friends with some upper-classmen. I didn't do particularly well in school, either socially or academically." His breath tickled my ear. "I had a fight with Lynn, and I left. It was stupid."

I turned my face toward him, putting us nose to nose. For a moment I could smell the fresh Scotch on his breath, and then he turned his ear toward me.

"When did you come back?" I asked and turned my head for the answer.

"Just over three weeks ago." The tickle in my ear was worse. It took an effort not to giggle. I started to turn my head toward him, but he pressed his mouth to my ear as if he were going to stick his tongue in it. "The university's alumni office kept track of me," he whispered, and the flesh on my arms broke into goose bumps. "I get the magazine. A couple of months ago, Derek and Lynn were featured in Alumni News. I looked her up."

I turned my head to whisper in his ear. "You look up Derek, too?" I turned my ear toward him for the answer.

"I didn't know him. I arranged a meeting with Lynn and found she wasn't happy. She was looking for a way out."

I assumed he meant "a way out of the marriage" and not that Lynn was contemplating suicide. He leaned forward and had another sip of his Scotch. I drank some water. When he sat back, I leaned into him and asked, "Where have you been meeting her? At the house?"

"No. I've never been in the house."

"There are no fingerprints for the police to find? You're sure?"

He hesitated, then leaned toward me. "There are outside stairs in back of the house that lead up to a porch off the master bedroom. I've been there." His cold lips and hot breath were causing my breathing to quicken.

"Where? Porch or bedroom?"

He hesitated. "Both."

"How many times in the bedroom?"

"Only once or twice, briefly. I may not have touched anything other than a doorknob or the frame of the door."

I took a breath and exhaled it. If the police looked—and the attention they were showing his hotel room suggested they would—they were going to find his fingerprints inside the house. When I turned my head toward him, I could see the man sitting alone behind us, his head turned toward the dance floor so that his left ear faced our direction. There was no way he could hear us over the sound of Nelly Furtado's chanting, but I put my mouth against Bruno's ear to ask, "What time did you leave there tonight?"

He drained his drink, then put his mouth on my ear. "I wasn't there tonight."

"I don't believe you," I whispered, my mouth moving against his ear. It was a heck of a way to question a witness, I thought.

Bruno shrugged, looked at me, tilted his head.

"Okay," I said in normal tones. "We'll go with that." I took his hand and stood up. When we had left the music of the nightclub and climbed the steps to the street, the soft sound of the rain on the cobblestones was like a profound silence. As we reached the sidewalk, the door below us opened again with a burst of music, and the man who had been sitting behind us came out. Ignoring him, I pulled at Bruno's hand and stepped into the street.

The woman whom I'd seen with the ice bucket on the fourth floor was sitting in the hotel lobby. She stood as we passed her and followed us toward the elevators. I pressed the button, and while we were waiting for the elevator, the man from The Tobacco Company joined us.

The doors slipped open, and the four of us stepped in.

"Where to?" I asked, my hand hovering in front of the panel of buttons.

The woman and the man exchanged glances. "Four," the woman said.

I pushed four, and the cab started up.

"I'm Robin Starling," I said. "I think I've seen you around."

The woman shrugged.

"This is Steve Bruno," I said.

The man from The Tobacco Company nodded.

"We're going to his room now. I'm not sure what will develop, but perhaps you'd like to come in and pull up chairs."

Again, the man and woman looked at each other. "Perhaps we will," the man said.

I smiled at him.

"What are you doing?" Bruno said to me.

"Trying to add a little spice to my love life."

His lip curled in evident disgust. He had a low threshold.

The elevator doors slid open on the fourth floor, and the four of us filed out and down the hall. We stopped in front of Bruno's door. He got out his wallet and extracted his cardkey.

"Are you sure about this?" he said to me, rolling his eyes toward the man and woman who were standing with us.

I nodded, and he shrugged. "It's your show."

As he put the cardkey into the slot and pulled it out again, I said to the others, "It amazes me sometimes what men will do to please me."

Nobody even smiled. Bruno opened the door, and the other couple pushed past us. One glanced into the bathroom; the other stopped and stuck her head in the closet. We followed them in.

On the far side of the king-sized bed, the woman turned and said, "Where are they?"

"Where are who?" I asked, stopping beside Bruno.

"You know who."

"Is this one of those 'who's on first' kind of jokes?" When I didn't get a response, I said, "I think it's time we see some I.D."

The man pulled out a leather folder and showed me a badge.

"Wait a second, I want to see it." I took the folder from him. His name was Adam King. "You?" I said.

After a moment's hesitation, she produced her own identification. I studied it, then handed it back.

"Thank you, Stephanie," I said. "Now perhaps you can tell us what you want."

"We want the Nolans."

I assumed that the police knew who I was and that playing dumb would be counterproductive. "Their rooms are on the third floor," I said. "I called up when I first got here and talked to Matt."

"They're not in their rooms."

"Well, they're not in here," I said.

Adam toed the wooden frame beneath the bedspread. There weren't a lot of potential hiding places.

"What did you do with them?" Stephanie said.

"I just got here," I said. "I walked in with you. Remember?"

She looked at Bruno, who looked back, but didn't speak. Her eyes fastened on the connecting door to room 439, and she strode to it and pulled it open to reveal the blank door on the other side. She knocked on it.

We all waited, but she didn't get an answer.

She went to the bedside table, picked up the receiver, and dialed a number. "Hi," she said. "This is Stephanie Hoard of the Richmond Police Department. Could you tell me if room 439 is occupied? Uh huh. Thank you." She hung up and glared at me.

"What did I do?" I asked.

To Adam, she said, "It's rented to a Brooke Marshall."

The name, evidently, didn't mean anything to either of them.

"Unless you have a warrant, I think it's time you left," I said.

Stephanie's mouth tightened. She left the hotel room, and I followed her closely enough to catch the door as she knocked on the door directly across from Bruno's. It was opened by a man I hadn't seen before. They engaged in a whispered conversation, then Stephanie went to room 439 and banged on the door with the heel of her fist. She hit the door three times, waited, then hit it three more times. I wondered whether Lynn and Matt were sitting on the bed, paralyzed with dread, or whether they were trying to conceal themselves in the closet or behind the shower curtain.

Much to my surprise, the door to room 439 opened. Brooke was there, her hair tousled. She was wearing a white terrycloth bathrobe with the name of the hotel stitched on the breast. Her expression, as she looked at Stephanie, was incredulous.

"What is wrong with you? It's the middle of the night," she said. Seeing the rest of us, she asked, "Is something the matter? Is there a fire?"

Stephanie held up her badge. "We'd like to search your room," she said.

"What for?"

"May we come in?"

Brooke looked suddenly angry. "Do you have a warrant?"

"Do we need to get one?"

"I think you do."

"What have you got to hide?"

"Nothing to hide, but lots to protect," Brooke said. "You can't just…"

Stephanie's cell phone began playing a song by Green Day. She stepped back and pulled it off her belt. "Hoard," she said, giving her last name.

She listened.

"Son of a gun," she said. After a moment she flipped the phone closed. To Adam she said, "The Nolans are back in their room. John just saw them going in."

"Where have they been?"

She rolled her eyes. "We know where they've been."

"Where do they say they've been?"

"For a walk." She jerked her head at Bruno and me, who were standing together. "Let's take one ourselves."

The man who had been in the room across from Bruno's said, "They didn't come out that door." He pointed at the door of Bruno's room.

"Well, they sure got out somehow."

Chapter 6

"How did you get them out?" I asked Brooke. It was an hour later, and we were headed once again out the Downtown Expressway toward I-64.

"I took a chance," Brooke said. "When I heard all those people in Bruno's room, I checked the corridor. It looked empty to me, so I sent the Nolans high-tailing it toward the stairwell at the opposite end of the hall from the elevators."

"We were lucky." I brought her up to date, telling her everything I'd learned from the Nolans and from Steve Bruno. She'd already heard some of it from Lynn and Matt.

"I don't see that the hocus pocus at the hotel matters much," she said, taking the ramp onto I-64. "If Matt Nolan could establish that Lynn and Steve Bruno were old sweethearts, then the police can."

"Sure, but nothing would bring it home to the jury like finding her in his hotel room the night of her husband's murder."

"Can't the police still testify about seeing her go into his room?"

"Sure, but they'd also have to admit that she wasn't there an hour or so later and that they never saw her leave. I think it muddies the waters enough that the prosecution will leave it alone."

Brooke drove for a while in silence. "So Steve Bruno showed up three weeks ago and has been seeing Lynn on the sly," she said at last.

"You think there's a romantic angle?" I asked her.

"Don't you?"

I didn't know. "There doesn't have to be," I said. "It could be an old friend helping out in tough times."

"When do you think Derek popped her in the eye?"

"Yesterday?" I checked my watch. "Day before yesterday," I amended. "The discoloration was already pretty far advanced yesterday morning."

"So he pops her in the eye, and within twenty-four hours someone's shot him in the head."

"And we have an old boyfriend going in and out of the master bedroom," I said.

"It looks bad. It's plain neither Derek's wife nor his kid will miss him much."

"True. Somehow I can't see either one of them as a killer, though."

"Would you know a killer if you saw one?"

"Maybe. The embezzler's our best candidate—big beefy guy with a bald head."

"Oh yes, clearly a killer." After a bit she added, "Why, though? Revenge for being canned?" She exited the interstate in the far West End.

"The motive is stronger than that. Derek's murder may save him from criminal prosecution. Walker goes in, shoots Derek Nolan, takes the forged notes from the drawer, and he's home free. The file drawer was open, remember."

"He risks prosecution for murder to cover up an embezzlement?" Brooke asked.

"He might not have expected to run into Melissa Butler on the way out. If Walker was the man she saw."

"And if the man she saw was the killer."

I sighed. "I know. All we know for sure is that she saw a man leaving the scene."

"And we don't know if he matches Walker's description or Bruno's or somebody else's entirely."

"I'd sure like to ask her some questions about that."

"Be nice if you'd questioned her while you had her," Brooke said.

"Who knew she was about to disappear? I didn't have any reason to question her, anyway. Everyone was telling me Derek was the one who had knocked her down. By the time I knew that was impossible, I had a corpse to think about and a client who was intent on tampering with the evidence."

"Now that's what's interesting," Brooke said. "Why would she do that? She's obviously protecting someone."

"Why do you say that?"

"Think about it. Someone's murdered her husband. She has no idea who or why. Depending on the motivation, she or her son could be the next target, and yet all she cares about is obstructing the police investigation."

"Doesn't make sense, does it?" I said.

"Not unless she has a pretty good idea who did it, and why."

"Or at least who might be accused of doing it."

Brooke nodded and turned onto our street. "I think we have a pretty good idea of who's going to be accused of doing it."

"Steve Bruno?"

"Or Lynn herself. Maybe both."

"Well, as soon as Melissa Butler turns up, we'll have a chance to straighten things out. Either she saw Bruno, and he's cooked, or she saw somebody else. Whoever she saw is going to be the number-one suspect."

"You're assuming Melissa Butler is going to turn up," Brooke said.

"She better turn up. She has my car, and my wallet's under the front seat."

Chapter 7

The next morning, the police arrested Lynn Nolan and Steve Bruno for the murder of Derek Nolan. I got Lynn's call at the office just as I was preparing to leave for lunch.

"Don't answer questions," I told her. "Don't say anything about your family or about Bruno or about anything you did yesterday." I was on my feet behind my desk, trying to think, my hand gripping the receiver so hard that it was becoming painful.

"They found a gun," she said. "In a shoebox in my closet."

Of course they did. "This isn't the time to talk about it. I'll come see you this afternoon."

"I didn't put it there. I'd never seen the gun before."

"We'll talk about it later, as early in the afternoon as I can make it."

"I want you to represent both of us. Steve and me."

"I can't," I said automatically.

"They claim we did it together."

It might mean that she and Bruno had no conflict of interests, but a conflict of interests was something I didn't want to come within a mile of. "I'll think about it," I said. "Which one do they say pulled the trigger?"

"They've told it to me both ways. I don't think they care."

I hung up, and the phone rang again. I reached for it, then stopped dead, my hand on the receiver. The LCD read "Starling, Charles." It was my father. The phone rang four times, then switched the caller to voice mail. I sat with my hand still on the receiver, waiting for the red message light to appear.

Behind me, a voice said, "You ready?" and I spun in my chair.

John Parker, another of the firm's associate attorneys, stood in my doorway.

"You ready?" he said again.

"For what?" My heart was still pounding.

"Aren't we going to lunch?"

We were. Not too long before Lynn's phone call he'd called to ask, and I'd agreed, somewhat against my better judgment. I had something of a history with John, and I still found any time spent with him to be charged with possibilities. For me John Parker wasn't quite safe.

"I'm not hungry," I said.

"Ten minutes ago you were starving."

"I have meat to eat ye know not of."

John frowned at me, looking perplexed.

"It's the Bible," I said. "The last few times I've stayed in a hotel, I've read bits of the one in the nightstand."

"I know it's the Bible. Are you saying you've been witnessing to Samaritans?"

59

Evidently, John knew the Bible better than I did. "I got a phone call," I said. Actually two phone calls. I glanced back at the phone, but Dad hadn't left a message. "I'm about to be involved in my second criminal case."

'Uh oh." He came into the office and dropped into a chair across the desk from me. "As attorney or defendant?"

I felt one corner of my mouth lifting. "Attorney," I said.

"Better than the alternative, but Larsen's not going to like it." Dick Larsen was the firm's senior partner.

"I know. That's what's happened to my appetite."

"Just don't handle it like you did the last one."

"In the last one I was representing you," I said.

My phone rang yet again, but the tone this time indicated an internal call. It was the receptionist.

I picked up. "Starling."

"A Sergeant Jordan is on his way back."

"Crap," I said.

"Pardon?" she said.

"I mean, thank you." I put the receiver back in its cradle and turned to John. "Sergeant James Jordan is…" It was too late. Jordan was in the hallway, visible through the glass wall of my office. The glass walls were the thing I hated most about working at Northcutt, Hambrick and Larsen. The partners had offices with opaque walls along the perimeter of the ninth and tenth floors. The associates were clustered in the interior, each in his or her own goldfish bowl.

John turned as Jordan stopped in the open doorway.

"Mr. Parker," Jordan said.

John stood warily, keeping his gaze fixed on Jordan. "Officer Jordan," he said.

"You two still thick as thieves?" Jordan nodded at me. "Hello, Robin."

"I'll see you," John said to me. Jordan stepped aside for him and watched him stride off down the hall.

Jordan came in and sat down. "Nervous fellow," he said, jerking his head in the direction John had gone.

"How come he's Mr. Parker, and I'm just Robin?" I asked.

Jordan smiled. "I guess I don't like him as well as I do you."

"At least this time you're not here to arrest him."

"No, this time it's you I'm after."

"Me?"

"We found your car. It was parked along the curb near the Greyhound station. The meter had expired."

"So I've got a ticket?"

"The car's been impounded. I'm afraid it will cost you something to get it back."

"You're kidding me."

"I'm afraid not. One-eighty in towing charges."

I was incredulous. "One hundred eighty dollars? If you'd just called me, I'd have come and gotten it."

He gave me a shrug and a smile that might have been apologetic. "By the time I knew anything about it, it was too late."

I sat back in my chair, disgusted. Finally, I said, "Well, where is Melissa? What does she have to say for herself?"

"Nothing. We still can't find her."

"Did she take a bus out of town? Where'd she go?"

"Evidently nowhere, at least not by bus."

"That's interesting. Has she been back to her apartment?"

"No."

"Where did she go then? What was the car doing at the bus station?"

"I was hoping you could tell me. Evidently, somebody picked her up outside the station."

"Taxi?"

He shook his head.

"Well, I didn't do it. I didn't have a car."

"She left the murder scene in your car."

"I've explained that. Look, I'm the last person to want to hide Melissa Butler. I'm desperate for some kind of description of the man who knocked her down."

"Are you? Maybe you didn't like what she had to say, and that's why Melissa's gone missing."

"You've made that accusation before," I said. "I'm not going to keep denying it."

"You talked to her. I didn't. It just seems odd you'd have let her go without getting a description out of her."

"I didn't let her go. I thought I was dealing with domestic violence. Everybody else in that house did, too. I had no idea she was about to take off."

"I'm just telling you how it looks," Jordan said. "They tell me the district attorney is mad as a wet hen. If much more turns up in the way of evidence, you could be losing your license to practice law."

"Well, I don't know what I can do about it." I thought about it, and my mouth twitched. "Did somebody really compare Aubrey Biggs to a wet hen?"

Jordan stood up. "I take it you know we've arrested Lynn Nolan and Steve Bruno for the murder."

"I just got the phone call."

"So I'll be seeing you. A lot, maybe." He raised a hand to me as he turned toward the door.

"Wait." I snatched my purse from the desk drawer, more for appearances than anything, since my wallet had been in my car, and went around the desk after him. "I need a ride to the impound lot, or wherever the heck they've taken my car."

Chapter 8

My wallet was still where I had put it, tucked underneath the front seat. After I'd written my check and signed the necessary papers, I called Brooke on her cell phone. "Where are you?" I asked when she picked up, knowing she was often on site at some company or other. She was an information systems manager who recently had begun working out of the house as a consultant.

"At home. I've got an appointment, though, in a little over an hour. Where are you?"

"Just leaving the impound lot. They found my car."

"Where?"

I told her about it and about the arrest of Steve Bruno and Lynn Nolan. "What I'd like to do now is have my car dusted for prints."

"Fingerprints? You mean Melissa's fingerprints?"

"Yes. I want to find her."

"The police didn't dust it?"

"I don't know, and I don't want to ask. What I'm hoping is that we can find a detective agency that can lift the prints and check the databases to see if Melissa Butler has a record somewhere."

"A criminal record? What makes you think that?"

"Her disappearance. It seems to be voluntary, and I'm looking for a reason."

"Aren't the police looking for one, too?"

"The police already have their reason. They think I engineered her disappearance so she wouldn't identify Steve Bruno. I know I didn't, so I'm one up on them. Can you call a few detective agencies for me while I'm at the jail talking to my clients?"

"Plural?"

"I'm thinking about it."

"Suppose you could get Lynn off by implicating Bruno?"

"That would be the problem. I don't think she'd want me to do it, though."

"It's your law license. I'll check out the detective agencies for you."

"Thanks, Brooke. Bye."

I punched the phone off and dropped it back into my purse.

When I saw Lynn in the visitor's room, she looked as if she hadn't gotten a lot of sleep. Her face had that splotchy look that blondes sometimes get under stress.

"How are you holding up?" I asked her when she had taken her seat across the table from me.

"Better than I would have expected."

"Tell me about the gun they found."

"It was in a shoebox in my closet."

"Yes, you said that."

"I didn't put it there."

"And you've never seen it before and you don't know whose it is," I said.

She looked at me without expression.

"Is that right?" I said.

She nodded.

"What have the police told you about the case against you?"

"Just the gun. And they asked me about my black eye."

"What did you tell them?"

"Nothing. You told me not to."

I had told her, but hadn't really expected her to listen. "Good job," I said. "Did they ask you about your movements yesterday?"

"Yes, but I didn't tell them anything."

"Did they focus on any particular time period?"

"The evening from about five o'clock on."

"What were you doing?"

"Reading a Stephanie Plum novel until Matt got home. Then I got him some dinner."

"What did you have?"

"Meatloaf. With green beans and mashed potatoes."

"I think it would be better for you and Steve to each have your own lawyer," I said, changing the subject.

"No," she said, some energy coming into her voice and posture for the first time. "I don't want to get off at Steve's expense. And he doesn't want to hire a lawyer to try to pin the crime on me."

I looked at her thoughtfully.

"It's all or nothing," she said. "I won't lose him again."

"What time did he leave the house last night?"

"He..." She stopped. "He wasn't there."

"But he has been there. He's come and gone through the balcony off your bedroom."

"No, he hasn't."

"Lynn. He told me he had. Fingerprint evidence is going to prove it."

"Why are you asking me then? Are you trying to trap me?"

"I'm trying to find out what happened. I have to know what we're up against."

She didn't answer.

"Lynn?"

She got to her feet. "You'll have to do the best you can," she said.

I stood, too. "I'm on your side. You believe that, don't you?"

She hesitated, then moved her head in a quick, birdlike nod.

"Then why won't you talk to me?"

"I can't tell you anything that will help us."

"Don't think about what will help. Just give me the facts, and I'll do what I can with them."

She gave me a sickly smile and turned away.

"Lynn said you were at the house last night," I told Bruno. He looked better than Lynn did, though his skin had a sheen to it.

His eyes narrowed. "No, she didn't."

"Are you denying you were there?"

"I don't think I like your methods," he said.

Join the club, I thought. "I've been driven to them," I said. "I have a couple of clients who for some reason are being selective in what they tell me. It's bad for the quality of your representation."

"That's our call, isn't it?"

"It's also bad to have one lawyer representing two defendants who might develop opposing interests."

"They seem to think we acted in concert," Bruno said. "I think they're going to try us together."

"Suppose your lawyer could sell the jury on the possibility that Lynn acted alone? It would get you off the hook."

He shook his head, his expression decisive. "I wouldn't want that."

"You'd rather die?"

"If that's the alternative."

"It's not just a figure of speech here," I said. "Virginia has the death penalty. If this goes to trial, it will be because the prosecution thinks it can get a conviction."

He didn't say anything to that.

"The way I understand it, both of you want me to represent both of you."

"Why not?" he said.

"Even if you want to use the same lawyer, you might want to look around for someone with more experience. I've only had one capital murder case in my career."

"How did it go?"

"I got the case tossed out at the preliminary hearing, but that may have been a fluke."

His mouth stretched. "We could use a fluke like that."

I gave up.

Chapter 9

Brooke had left a name for me on voicemail: Rodney Burns. His agency was on the back side of a strip mall on West Broad Street. I stopped my car in a parking space in front of the agency—all the spaces were empty—and sat staring dubiously at the Venetian blinds that hung inside the glass walls from ceiling to floor. Some of the blinds hung crookedly, and some were bent, giving the place a dilapidated appearance. Only the lettering on the door looked professionally done: Rodney Burns, Detective Agency.

I got my cell phone out and started to call Brooke, then didn't. She was probably at her meeting. Anyway, she'd looked up the place in a phone book or on the Internet and wouldn't know anything about Mr. Burns other than his address and phone number. I got out of my Beetle.

When I yanked at the door, I found it wasn't locked, though I'd half-expected it to be. It opened into the outer of two offices. The only thing in it was a long computer table with a phone on it—no computer—and a secretarial chair with the back canted sideways.

A glass wall blocked off the inner office, the bottom panes, each about three feet square, painted white. A man's head popped above the painted portion, and I yelped.

"Sorry," he said. "Sorry." His body turned a bit as he moved toward the doorway on the other side of the glass, but his eyes never left me, as if he feared I might vanish if he took his eyes off me.

"I'm Robin Starling," I said, when he got to the doorway.

"Yes," he said. "The lawyer?"

"A lawyer. I think there's more than one."

"Yes. Your associate called about you."

"Brooke Marshall?"

"Yes. That was the name." He had thinning hair combed over a domelike head, and a thin mustache to go with it. His brown suit looked as though he might have slept in it.

"I'm here about…"

"Fingerprints," he said, nodding at me. "You want your car dusted for fingerprints."

"That's right. The person who left the prints is a redhead about five-four or so, somewhere in her twenties, and her name may or may not be Melissa Butler."

He came forward, stopping close enough to me that he had to look up. "Your prints are on the car?"

"I assume so."

"We'll have to take them for purposes of elimination." He turned away from me and went back into the inner office, where he bent down and disappeared behind the painted panes of glass.

His head popped into view again. "Got it," he said. "Right in here."

I went to the doorway. A big desk with peeling laminate dominated the small inner office. Magazines and folders were stacked along one wall, and papers were scattered over the desk. He opened a bottle and poured a little ink onto a rectangular sheet of glass, spread the ink with a roller, and, setting the roller on a stack of paper towels, looked up at me expectantly.

"I'm not sure I like this," I said.

"You'd like it less if I sent your prints around to a bunch of law enforcement agencies, asking for identification," he said.

I nodded unwillingly, and he held out his hand for mine. "The sooner begun, the sooner done," he said. The expression seemed too old for him by about thirty years, assuming him to be on the youthful side of fifty. I stepped forward, though, and didn't pull away when he reached out matter-of-factly and took my hand.

"Just relax," he said. "Let me do the work." He rolled my index finger on the inky glass and then onto a large white card. He worked efficiently and had all ten fingers done in about a minute. "Now. Let's do all eight fingers at once. Just touch them to the glass, then press them into these boxes at the bottom of the card here. Okay, now the thumbs." He handed me a paper towel. "Wipe the worst of that off, then I'll give you a squirt of cleaner."

The ink came off easily, much more easily than I expected.

"Now let's take a look at your car," he said.

We went out.

"How long did this person have your car?"

"Not long, a few hours."

"So we're looking at the steering wheel, the gearshift, the leather seats, the dash…" He moved around the car. "Maybe the exterior of the trunk and around the door handles."

"Okay," I said.

He went back inside and came back with a plastic-sided briefcase. I stood and watched him work with his dark powder and his big, fluffy brush. He put white tape over the prints he found and scribbled a cryptic notation on the back of each piece, presumably to record the location of the print. Then he lifted the prints and attached them to a sticky sheet of cardboard. To a novice like me, it looked as if he knew what he was doing.

"I'll photograph them inside," he said. "I'll get better results that way."

"Okay."

In less than an hour from the time I'd pulled up, I was on the road again. I drove back downtown to the office, where I found I had three missed phone calls, but no voicemail. I checked the phone's directory to see who had called. The answer was Starling, Charles. My father had called three times without leaving a message. Maybe he had something serious to tell me, and he didn't think I would call him back. He was right about that.

With an effort, I put Starling Charles out of my mind, and I managed to spend the rest of the afternoon on the commercial litigation the firm paid me to do.

Chapter 10

Brooke got home shortly after I did. She was wearing a casual, olive suit with matching pumps. The color went well with her red hair.

"Client?" I said.

"West End Pool Supplies."

"Must be important. You're wearing nylons."

She looked down at her legs, turning her right foot. "They say they're coming back, but I don't know."

The thought made me shudder. "I hate pantyhose," I said.

"Me, too." She lifted the hem of her skirt far enough to let me see the black garters.

I gave her a look. "There's a man at West End Pool, isn't there?" I said.

"Quite a few of them. They've got stores now from Ashland to St. Petersburg, which is why they need me to improve their inventory management."

"You know what I mean. There's one particular man."

She gave me a shrug and a half smile.

"And I'll bet he got a glimpse of those garters at some point today."

She headed out of the living room, saying over her shoulder, "It doesn't hurt to give a man something to think about."

"Are you kidding?" I called, following her. "It's all men do think about. If they suspect for a moment that you're naked underneath your clothes, they can't focus on anything else."

She laughed, shrugging out of her jacket and getting a hanger from the closet.

"I'll let you get changed, then I've got a proposition for you," I said.

"Sorry to disappoint you, but I'm straight."

I held up my hands and turned back down the hall.

When she joined me in the living room, she was wearing jeans and a polo shirt, which was what I was wearing. "Okay," she said. "What's the proposition? Actually, first tell me how Rodney Burns worked out."

I muted the television. "He worked out okay, I think. Time will tell."

"That's a ringing endorsement. So what's your proposition?"

"I'll buy you dinner if you'll go with me to visit a potential witness," I said.

"Who's the witness?"

"Liz Lockard, Derek Nolan's former secretary. She lives in a house on Three Chopt Road not far from the Country Club."

"Is that where the dinner is?"

"At Liz's house?"

"The Country Club."

"I was thinking Fuddruckers."

"You're offering me a hamburger?"

"Long John Silvers?"

She laughed. "It's getting worse," she said. "I'll go with the hamburger."

When we got to the restaurant, though, she decided to have a grilled chicken sandwich instead. I had the burger, but forewent the cheese and, at the last moment, talked myself out of a milkshake to go with it. Being five-eleven and a runner, I get away with a lot, but every girl has her limits.

Liz Lockard's house was a split-level dating from the 1950s. It had gleaming shutters and a nice lawn, though the car in her driveway was an old Civic with dulled paint.

Brooke and I went up the short sidewalk, mounted the stoop, and rang the bell. We waited and rang again. "I guess you didn't call before we came," Brooke said.

"If I'd done that, nobody would have been here, and it would have been on purpose." I pointed to the car. "But I think somebody's here."

"Somebody could have picked her up. Boyfriend maybe."

"It's possible," I conceded. Matt Nolan had seen Liz at the horse track with Mark Walker, which might mean he was her boyfriend if no one else was. "Let's take a closer look at the car."

"Who are you?" a voice said from inside the front door.

We turned back. "I'm Robin Starling," I said. "I'm investigating the murder of your former employer, Derek Nolan."

There was a sharp click, and the door opened to the length of its safety chain. A woman's face was visible through the crack, one with close-cut, straw-colored hair and a reddish complexion. "I thought you guys had already made an arrest," she said. Her voice was unexpectedly deep.

I smiled. "We guys work fast."

Brooke said, "We're always looking for additional evidence to bolster our case."

I wondered that anyone could mistake us for cops in our jeans and topsiders, but the chain came off the door, and we followed Liz into her living room. She had a squarish physique and a charging gait, even over the short distance from her front door to a living room easy chair. Her brush-cut, blond hair had dark roots.

When we were all seated, she asked, "Can I get you something to eat, drink, smoke, or chew?"

"That opens up some possibilities," I said.

Her laugh was like a donkey's bray.

I glanced at Brooke. "Why don't we get right to it?" I said. "How long did you work for Derek Nolan?"

Her eyes went from me to Brooke and back again. "Two years," she said. "A little more."

"How long did Mark Walker work for him?"

She shook her head. "Longer than that. Somewhere between five and ten years, I think."

"Until when?"

"A week and a half ago, two weeks. Mr. Nolan fired him for what he said was embezzlement."

"Wasn't it?"

"I don't know. Mr. Nolan said Walker forged a note."

"How did that work?"

"Somebody paid off his note early." She stopped talking, as if reconsidering how much she was prepared to tell us.

"And...," Brooke prompted.

"And Walker marked the note paid and gave it back to the borrower," I said, when Liz didn't respond. "And printed off another one for the files. Is that how it worked?"

"That's what he said."

"What Mr. Nolan said?"

She nodded.

"Is collecting money part of Mr. Walker's job?"

"Sometimes."

"He works there in the office? Where were you when this borrower came in and paid off his note?"

"It was Wednesday, my afternoon off. I work a half-day on Saturday."

"And Mark Walker fills in for you on Wednesday afternoons?"

She shrugged. "Not usually." A fount of information she wasn't.

"But he was there that afternoon," I said.

"I don't know. The debtor told Mr. Nolan it was some man."

There it was again: *some man* without any qualifiers or description. "Could you tell us what Mark Walker looks like?"

She shrugged. "He's a large man. Bald, except for a fringe of hair around his head."

"Dark hair?"

"Medium brown."

"How much money was missing?" Brooke asked.

"A little over sixteen thousand dollars," Liz said, turning to her.

I asked, "Who do you think might have taken it, if not Mr. Walker?"

"Mrs. Nolan might have done it."

"Mrs. Nolan?"

"If she needed it."

"Why would she need it?"

"Mr. Nolan didn't give her a lot of spending money, and what he gave her she had to account for. He kept her on a pretty tight leash."

I nodded thoughtfully.

"And she had that old boyfriend hanging around. He could have been the man who took the money from the client."

"Would he have known enough about the system to find the debtor's promissory note in the files and to print a duplicate?"

"It isn't that complicated."

"What old boyfriend was this?" Brooke asked.

"Somebody named Steve. I never saw the man, but I understand Mrs. Nolan actually had him in the house. Mr. Nolan seemed pretty upset about it in that cold way of his."

"It seems indiscreet for Mrs. Nolan to have him in the house," I said.

"Especially since Mr. Nolan worked out of it," Brooke added.

"There's a back way into the second floor—a wooden staircase up to the balcony off the master bedroom. The basement apartment only opens to the front of the house. If Derek...Mr. Nolan...came in the front door, there'd be plenty of time to slip out the back."

"Be easy enough to catch them at it, though, if Mr. Nolan became suspicious."

"He did catch them at it. Hired a detective and everything. He didn't know who the boyfriend was until the detective found Steve-o's cell phone." Liz smiled unpleasantly.

"Steve-o?" Brooke asked.

"That's what Mr. Nolan started calling him after he found the phone. He was going to confront his wife with it."

"But evidently he didn't," I said. "At least not right away."

"He wanted the circumstances to be just right. He was engineering a showdown, was the way he put it."

I thought of the cell phone that had been in the right hand of Derek's corpse. Maybe there had been a showdown, one Derek had engineered too well. The doorbell rang, and my heart jumped into my chest.

Brooke looked at me; I looked from her to Liz Lockard, who was looking apprehensive. I wondered if we were about to meet the large and imposing Mr. Walker.

Liz went to the door, but slowly. She didn't charge at it this time. She opened it, and we heard voices. Liz came back in, and there were two cops on her heels, James Jordan and his partner Ray Hernandez.

"Good grief," Jordan said when he saw us.

"Officer Jordan," I said, getting to my feet.

"What are you doing here?"

"I wasn't getting copies of your reports, so I thought I'd better get out and do a little investigating of my own."

Liz was looking back and forth between us. "You mean she's not one of you?" she said, looking at Jordan and jerking her head at me. "She's not a cop?"

"Did she tell you she was a cop?"

"Sure she did. She…" Liz trailed off.

"She said we were investigating the murder of Derek Nolan," Brooke said.

Hernandez said to Liz, "She's the attorney representing Lynn Nolan and Steve Bruno."

Liz looked at me with sudden dislike. "Well, what I have to say doesn't help her clients much."

"I appreciate your talking to me anyway," I said.

"I don't have anything more to say to you."

Jordan said, "In that case, let me get the door for you, Ms. Starling." He went to the front door and held it open. Brooke went out first. As I went by him, he said, "You're playing close to the edge, Robin."

"What? I'm not allowed to investigate? Who made those rules?"

He closed the door on us without answering.

I looked at Brooke, and she shrugged.

Chapter 11

When we were back in my car, I said, "I think we're down to two possibilities. Either my clients are guilty, or the murder is connected to Mark Walker's embezzlement."

"If he was guilty of the embezzlement. 'Some man' could mean Steve Bruno."

"We should have asked where Walker lives." I started the car and backed down the driveway.

"The phone book might tell us," Brooke said. "Or Derek might have a personnel file for him."

"It would also be nice to talk to the borrower who paid off early. He should be able to describe the man he gave the money to."

"Maybe we can get the name of the borrower from Nolan's files."

I nodded. "Maybe. Are you up for a trip down to Church Hill?"

"Sure."

"I think Matt Nolan is back home. He can let us in."

"Is he living there by himself now that his mother's been arrested?"

"I think so."

"That must be pretty hard on him."

She may have been right. When Matt answered the door at the top of the steps, his hair stuck up in front, and his cheek had parallel lines imprinted on it as if he had spent the afternoon sleeping on his face. He brightened when he saw us, though, and stepped back from the door by way of invitation.

As we went past him into the living room, he asked, "Is there any news?"

"No," I said.

"Oh."

"But I have talked to your mother. She seems to be holding up."

He nodded, his eyes moving back and forth between us. "For a moment I thought you were Melissa," he said to Brooke.

"Thicker hair, fewer freckles," I said, describing Brooke.

Brooke smiled at him. "Sorry."

He shrugged, and his eyes stayed on her face.

"Nobody's seen Melissa," I said. "According to the police, she hasn't been back to her apartment."

"What are they doing to find her?"

"Harassing me."

He looked surprised.

"Their theory seems to be that I've got her socked away somewhere because I don't want her to identify Steve Bruno."

"That's ridiculous."

"Her driving away in my car just before homicide got here is what gave them the idea. That, and they think I'm a loose cannon because of a few things I did in a previous case."

"What things?"

82

"Nothing worth talking about. The reason we stopped by was to take a look at your dad's office. Have the police finished with it?"

"Call him Derek. I've started thinking of him that way. If he's not my dad..." He trailed off.

"You'd rather be Bruno's son?"

"I'll never be anybody's son, but at least I won't be victimized any longer by Derek Nolan."

"You don't find you're missing him, just a little?"

He laughed shortly. "The air in this place was always too thick to breathe," he said. "It's like a heavy cloud's been lifted."

I gave him what I meant to be a sympathetic smile. "Your...Derek's office?" I said. "Can we look at it?"

He shrugged. "Sure. The police didn't tell me to keep out when they left this time. I'll get the key."

The office was as I remembered it, except that the high-backed desk chair was now standing upright and obscuring the computer monitor. As I approached the desk, I looked for blood on the floor beyond it, but there wasn't any. No hint of a stain on the thick Persian carpet, nothing at all to indicate the police had been there, or a corpse before them.

"Are you looking for something the police missed?" Matt asked me.

"No. I'm looking for something the police never looked for in the first place. I want to know who the debtor was in the Walker embezzlement. You don't know, do you?"

He shook his head. "I don't think I ever heard the name. Liz would know."

"We didn't get a chance to ask her."

"You've been to see her?"

I nodded.

"The police interrupted us," Brooke said.

I sat at the desk and opened the file drawer I'd seen open when we discovered Nolan's corpse. Though the drawer was equipped with a lock, the lock wasn't engaged, and the drawer slid open smoothly to reveal a neat row of manila folders nestled inside green hanging folders.

"Those are his active loans," Matt said. "The closed files are in that file cabinet." He pointed at a five-drawer lateral file cabinet in the corner.

"I guess the paid loan would be over there then."

He shrugged. "Walker didn't mark it paid, I don't think. That was the whole idea."

"But your…Derek had two weeks to move the file over."

"Except that he wasn't done with it. He was going to prosecute or whatever."

I opened the desk's middle drawer, where trays of pens, pencils, highlighters, paper clips, scissors, and a staple remover were neatly arranged. "Only one model of pen," I observed. "I've probably got a dozen kinds in my own desk." I closed the drawer and opened another. It held a phone book. The one below it held legal pads and nothing else. Mr. Nolan had been a neat, methodical man with the world's most uncluttered desk.

My hypothesis, for the moment, was that Mark Walker had killed Derek Nolan and taken the incriminating file. If that were the case, I was looking for something that wasn't there, which was going to make it difficult to find. "Who's managing the loan files now?" I asked Matt.

He shook his head. "Nobody."

"Liz Lockard?"

"I haven't seen her since..." He trailed off. "I haven't seen her for a couple of days."

"You or your mother fire her?"

"No, I don't think so. She just hasn't been coming in."

"That's interesting."

"She probably knows that neither mother nor I liked her much."

"Still, as far as we know, she doesn't have another source of income. Even if she didn't need the work, it would have been nice for her to offer her services."

Brooke said, "There was one thing I meant to ask her, but didn't get a chance. She evidently worked the day of the murder. What time did she leave?"

"I don't know," Matt said.

I nodded, my mind returning to the problem of collecting Nolan's outstanding loans. "Has anybody contacted you today about making a payment? How is that going to work?"

He shook his head. "Nobody's come by, and this phone doesn't ring up in the house."

I lifted the phone's handset and heard the stuttered dial tone that indicated voicemail. "Do you know Derek's password?" I asked.

Matt shook his head, and I frowned thoughtfully. "I'd better take the open files. I'll send out letters to the debtors and let them know where to make their payments. We'll keep track of the loans for you."

I got out a pen and a legal pad, then lifted a handful of files from the drawer. "They're alphabetized. That will make it easier." I started with the A's, writing just the last name of the debtor on the legal pad until I got to Johnson, which required a Johnson, D., a Johnson, M., and a Johnson, S. When I got to the second page of the legal pad, I suggested that Brooke and Matt could carry the files up to the car while I finished. Matt looked at Brooke and nodded quickly.

She gave him a smile. I smiled faintly to myself as I wrote "O'Sullivan, Parker, Peterson" in a column on the legal pad. There were, I thought, a lot of files, well over fifty.

I finished the second page and flapped it back to get a clean sheet, wondering what Nolan's average loan amount was. I opened the Peterson file and saw that the note, lying on top, had been made six months previously for 75,000 dollars. On the inside of the file folder was a column of dates with the amount $1520.73 written next to each. The last date was the fifteenth of this month, just over a week ago. Beneath the note was an amortization schedule, a financial statement for Michael Peterson, an appraisal of a building in downtown Richmond, and a photocopy of Peterson's tax return. I flipped back to the note and saw it was secured by the downtown building.

Brooke and Matt came back and stood waiting for me.

"Just a minute," I said. I counted the names I had written on my legal pad and the number of files I had left. There were fifty-eight. If 75,000 dollars was the average loan amount, then Nolan's loan portfolio was...I scribbled my calculations in the margin...4.35 million dollars. Of course, part of the Peterson note had been paid off. There was only about sixty-eight or sixty-nine thousand dollars outstanding. I checked the amortization schedule. After six payments, the balance was just under 68,700 dollars. I multiplied 69,000 by 58.

"A loan portfolio of about four million dollars," I said.

The interest rate on the Peterson loan was eight percent, which, multiplied by 4 million, yielded interest income of about 320,000 dollars per year. Of course, my calculations assumed that the Peterson file was typical of all fifty-eight loans in the active drawer, which was unlikely to be the case. Still, I thought I had some idea of the size of Nolan's operation.

Returning the Peterson file to the stack, I wrote Queen at the top of my new page and put that file on top of Peterson's. When I was done, I put the last file on the stack and turned the chair toward the walnut credenza and the computer on it. I turned the computer on and waited for it to boot. Brooke picked up the short stack of files, and Matt followed her to the door. There he took the files from her, then moved his head to indicate she should go first.

Uh oh, I thought, swiveling back to the computer. Matt was becoming infatuated, and him engaged to be married. On the other hand, his fiancée had disappeared, and Brooke looked a lot like her, though she was about five years older and in my opinion a lot prettier. I thought it might be what Freud called transference, though Psychology 101 was far enough behind me that I wasn't entirely sure transference was Freud's term and, if it was, what exactly he meant by it.

A box came up on the screen telling me to press Ctrl-Alt-Delete to enter a password. I hit the three buttons and the password box came up. I typed in

DEREK for the user name and LYNN for the password. It didn't work, so I tried DEREK and NNYL — Lynn backwards — then FACTOR and NNYL, then NOLAN with Lynn's name, both forward and backward. No luck.

I turned the chair and waited for Matt.

He came in behind Brooke, hanging back to let her go ahead of him, getting another smile in return.

"Matt," I said. "Do you know the password for this computer?"

He shook his head.

"Do you think your mother does?"

"I don't know."

"What's your birthday?" I tried several variations of that with the user names DEREK, FACTOR, and NOLAN, then I tried MATTHEW as the password, both forwards and backwards.

"This isn't going to work," I said.

"Try Derek-underscore-Nolan for the user name," Matt said.

"Okay." I typed it in, then looked up at him.

He hesitated. "Veronica Lynn," he said. "All lower case, no space."

I raised my eyebrows as I typed it in. The combination of user name and password worked. I was in.

"How many times have you been on this computer?" I asked, opening the My Documents folder.

He shook his head. "When I was little, he had a notebook computer he let me play games on. It had the same password."

There was a folder named Promissory Notes. Inside it there were hundreds of documents. I opened one named "Adams P." The document was a promissory note for 40 thousand dollars, prepared for the signature of one Paul Adams. It called for payments of one thousand dollars a month for two years with a balloon payment at the end.

"The date is just over five years ago," I said to Brooke and Matt, who were both looking over my shoulder. "I assume the note was paid off, but there's no indication of that in the document." I closed it and scrolled down to one named "Peterson R." I double-clicked it.

"Dated six months ago," Brooke said, reading over my shoulder.

"It was one of the files you carried out." Though the note was still outstanding, there was no indication of that in the file. It was just a note, ready to be printed and signed.

I closed the document and looked in My Recent Documents for an accounting file—something in QuickBooks or Peachtree. There wasn't one. There wasn't even a spreadsheet file.

"I don't think the computer's going to be very helpful."

Matt said, "Liz kept track of payments and sending past-due letters and stuff on her computer."

I turned the chair and looked at the computer sitting on the smaller desk by the door. "Ah," I said. I got up and moved to the other desk, and I turned on that computer. After a couple of minutes, the same box I'd seen on the other computer came up, telling me to press CTRL-ALT-DELETE. I did, and the box expanded to give me a place to enter a password.

"What do we do here?" I asked.

"Try the same thing," Matt said.

"Derek-underscore-Nolan?"

"Right, and Veronica Lynn."

It didn't work.

"Try Liz-underscore-Lockard."

"Then what?" I said as I typed it.

"Same password. Veronica Lynn."

That didn't work either.

"Liz-underscore-Lockard." He hesitated. "It's going to be his password. He's not going to let her lock up the computer with something personal to her."

"What's your middle name?" Brooke asked.

"Matthew. I'm James Matthew Nolan."

"We'll try James Matthew," I said, typing. "Eureka." The desktop appeared, the wallpaper a nonrepresentational smear of color. I looked in My Recent Documents and found what I was looking for, a Peachtree file.

"This is your department," I said to Brooke. "Can you print out reports that show loans outstanding, recent payments, and that sort of thing?"

She nodded. "I can do better than that." She pulled a lanyard from her purse that had a flash drive on the end of it. "I've got Peachtree on my computer at home. I'll just copy the file."

I gave her my place at the desk, and she made her copy.

"Get a copy of the notes on Derek's computer, too," I said. "Then I won't have to take it with me."

"What are you going to do with all of it?" Matt asked.

"For one thing, there's a business to manage. Somebody has to stay on top of this loan portfolio and see to it the money keeps coming in." I was thinking of Brooke, who had an undergraduate degree in accounting and a master's in information systems as well as a lot of practical experience. Not only could she do the Nolans some good, she'd just started out on her own and could use the work.

Matt nodded.

I said, "We may or may not be able to figure out which was the embezzlement file. If you could do a little looking around, it might prove helpful."

"Sure," he said.

"Something else I'm looking for is a personnel file on Mark Walker. I'm going to have to talk to him."

"I think he lives in Oregon Hill, up around Hollywood Cemetery somewhere." He sat at Lockard's desk, opened a file drawer, and started flipping through it. After a moment, I went to the file cabinet and opened a drawer. Brooke went to Nolan's desk. We gave up after thirty minutes.

If there had been a file on Walker, it wasn't there now.

Chapter 12

The next morning I got to the office as the receptionist was tucking her purse into the drawer of her desk. "Hello, Jennifer," I said as I stepped off the elevator.

"Hi, Robin." Our firm operated on a first-name basis except in the presence of clients.

"Anything new?"

She shook her head, and her dark hair bounced. She was a fresh-faced twenty-year-old to whom I'd once heard one of the (male) partners refer as "scenic," whatever that means. Out of the corner of my eye, I saw her pick up the phone as I turned down the hall.

I put my own purse in the desk drawer, punched the button to turn on my computer, and sat down. Pete Larsen, the firm's managing partner, appeared in my doorway. "Hello, Robin." He came in and sat in one of the client chairs.

"Hi, Pete."

"How's your practice going?"

"Can't complain." His go-slow approach had me bracing myself.

"What case is occupying you most right now?"

I moved my head. "One of our clients was murdered Monday," I said.

Larsen's eyebrows went up as if this were news to him.

"I did some estate planning for Derek and Lynn Nolan about a year ago," I said. "Then Monday morning Lynn showed up with her son to talk about divorce. Now she's in jail on a murder charge." I let one corner of my mouth rise in a half-smile. "There's a lot of variety in a law practice."

"Maybe too much variety," Larsen said. "We can't be all things to all people."

"No," I agreed.

After a brief silence, Larsen said, "Criminal law is very much its own specialty. It isn't the kind of thing you can dabble in with any degree of competence. A lot of things are that way. It's why we maintain our referral list." The referral list was a list of approved attorneys for different areas of law. I'd used it before when I couldn't take a case because of a conflict of interest.

Larsen cleared his throat. "Who have you referred the Nolan matter to?"

"I haven't referred it."

"Have you been talking to somebody about it? Which lawyer do you have in mind?"

"I guess I'd thought about handling it myself."

Larsen frowned. "I think that's a bad idea, Robin. Aside from the potential liability..."

"I think of myself as a trial lawyer," I said. "A trial lawyer is by nature a generalist."

"And a criminal lawyer is by nature a specialist."

"I sat in on some criminal trials when I was in law school," I said. "One of them was a capital case:

The defendant stabbed a fellow inmate in the state penitentiary. It didn't strike me as rocket science."

Larsen inhaled and exhaled, his nostrils flaring. "That's a different kind of defendant and a different kind of case."

"Are you telling me I'm incompetent? I've come up to speed in obstetrics and vasectomies for medical malpractice cases. I've boned up on securities law for…"

"This is different," Larsen said sharply.

I waited.

Larsen leaned forward. "Criminal defense is not something we want this firm associated with, particularly not in a potentially high profile case like this one." He sat back. "Don't make this any harder than it has to be, Robin. There are any number of lawyers we can hand this off to."

Rebellion rose in me, and I had to make an effort to control my respiration.

"Okay, Robin? Are we clear on this?" He sat forward, his hands on the arms of the chair.

"I understand you," I said.

"Good." He smiled at me.

I smiled back with an effort. He nodded at me, and I nodded back. Larsen left my office. The phone rang, and I picked it up. It was Rodney Burns.

"Ms. Starling?" he said.

"Yes."

"I wanted you to know I've eliminated your prints, and I have some inquiries underway concerning the rest of them."

"Thanks," I said.

"It will likely be tomorrow before I hear back from anyone. Tomorrow at the earliest."

"That's okay. Just let me know."

I dropped the phone back into its cradle and sat staring moodily at the corner of my desk. I could hear myself breathing.

I was still angry when Jennifer the backstabbing receptionist buzzed me to let me know I had a visitor. "A Charles Roberts," she said sweetly. "Shall I bring him back?"

I resisted the urge to ask why she hadn't followed precedent and sent him back without warning. "I'll come get him," I said.

He stood as I entered the reception area.

"Charles Robert Starling," I said.

"Hi, Robin." My father was still tall and straight, but he had lost weight and his hair had gone steel gray in the fifteen years since I had last seen him.

"Better come on back," I said.

I led the way, conscious of the too familiar stranger right on my heels. As he took a client chair, I walked around my desk to put it between us. When I turned, I found him studying me.

"So," I said. "I guess there's a reason you've begun harassing me?"

"Harassing you?"

"Calling repeatedly. Not leaving a message."

The ghost of a smile touched his face. "I didn't think you'd call me back."

I gave him a fierce smile in acknowledgment that he was probably right.

He took a breath and let it out again. "I would like to get reacquainted with my family," he said at last. "I've spoken to your mother and your brother."

"What about Jasmine?" She was the veterinary assistant he had run off with when I was sixteen.

"She's dead. Cervical cancer."

It knocked the breath out of me. She had been twenty-four or twenty-five, one of my favorite people before she had taken up with my father.

"It was a long fight," my father said. "She lasted almost two years after the first diagnosis. She died last month, the day after Labor Day."

I could see the strains of that fight still in his face. "Not quite what you signed on for, huh?"

He shook his head. "No. I traded everything for youth and energy and laughter..." He trailed off, looked away. "Even that turned hollow pretty quickly," he said. "Despite Jasmine's many fine qualities."

"But you stuck with her." The words were like dust in my mouth.

"By that time I didn't have anything else."

I stood. "Okay," I said.

He looked startled. "Okay?"

"That's enough for right now. I've got all I can process."

He got unwillingly to his feet. He was still a handsome man, though not as fit as I remembered him—thin rather than lean. He had aged more than the fifteen years that had passed. "Will I...May I call you again?"

"I'll call you," I said. "My phone got your number."

He looked at me a long time, and I met his gaze with an effort. He turned, finally, and left the office without saying anything else. I fell back exhausted into my chair, my eyes tracking him through the glass walls of my office until he disappeared from sight.

When I met Brooke for lunch, I didn't say anything about my father's visit. Even a mention would result in a lot of talk, and I simply wasn't up to it. We were at O'Riley's, a little restaurant on Grace Street just off the VCU campus. It was a narrow building with a cash register near the front and a row of booths on each side. When our waitress showed up to take our drink order, I asked, "Is Melissa working today?"

"Melissa Butler?"

"Yes," I said. "Redhead about your age?"

"Sure, I know Melissa, but she's not here. She's supposed to be. I heard she just didn't show up for work this morning."

"Was she here yesterday?"

"It was her day off. What can I get you to drink?"

"I'll have iced tea," I said.

The waitress looked at Brooke.

"Me, too."

"She got engaged recently to a boy named Matt," I said. "Maybe she took him home to show off to her family."

"Huh. Maybe." She gave me a mechanical smile and moved off.

"She really opened up to you, don't you think?" Brooke said.

"I found out Melissa didn't show up for work today."

"And didn't give notice. Yeah, that's something." She shifted in her seat and her khakis squeaked on the smooth vinyl.

The waitress brought our teas. I ordered a BLT on whole-wheat toast, and Brooke ordered a veggie wrap. None of us mentioned Melissa.

"After this we can go by her apartment," I said, taking the lemon slice off the edge of my glass and squeezing it into my tea. Brooke was stirring Splenda into hers.

"It was on Franklin, wasn't it?" she said. "Do you remember the number?"

"1313, apartment B," I said.

"Impressive."

"I called Matt just before I came and asked him."

"I should have known."

"Preparation as opposed to memorization," I said. I fished the key out of my purse and laid it on the table. "We can even get in. I swung by the house in Church Hill when I left the office."

"Matt had a key?"

"He's her fiancé. He wasn't real anxious to let go of it, but I managed to sweet-talk him."

The waitress showed up with our food. "Anything else?" she said. According to her nametag, her name was Rhonda.

"You don't like Melissa much, do you?" I asked.

Her eyebrows lifted, and her chin retreated into her neck. "Why do you say that?"

"It's okay," I said. "I don't like her much myself. Day before yesterday, she borrowed my car without permission. Not so much as a please or a thank you."

"Melissa takes care of Melissa."

"Do you know Matt Nolan? I understand they met right here in this restaurant."

"You're not just making casual conversation, are you?"

I moved my head equivocally.

"Who are you, and what do you want?"

Brooke said, "She can't help it, she's a lawyer. It's hard for her to sound like a human being."

"It's a struggle," I acknowledged. "I know the Nolans—Matt and his family. I'm just curious, I guess."

"So do your sandwiches look okay?"

I smiled at her. "They look fine, Rhonda. Thanks."

She moved off, and Brooke said, "You do have a knack."

"I do, don't I?"

Chapter 13

Franklin Street was a one-way street. We turned onto it at Stuart Circle, skirting the huge equestrian statue of J.E.B. Stuart. Melissa's apartment house was a large building with white paint that had flaked off in places to expose the red brick beneath. Franklin was parked up on both sides, so I went around the block, looking for a space along the curb. I finally found one about a block-and-a-half away.

"This close to VCU a lot of the tenants will be college students," Brooke said as we walked toward it. At one time the apartment house had been a single-family residence like many of the apartment buildings on this part of Franklin, but it had been cut up into apartments some decades before.

"Probably." The front door bore enough layers of old paint to give the wood a lumpy appearance, and it had warped in its frame so that I had to hit it with my shoulder to get it open. Inside, a narrow hallway ran right and left, seeming all the narrower because of the twelve-foot ceilings. Ahead of us, a staircase went up to a second floor.

We turned left into the hallway. In this wing were four apartments, two on each side of the hall. Apartment B was the first door on the left.

"Bingo," I said. I fitted the key into the deadbolt, and it slid back easily.

"Is this breaking and entering?" Brooke said.

"Not with the intent to commit a felony within."

"What does that have to do with it?"

"Even if we are breaking and entering, we're not committing burglary. And we do have the fiancé's permission." I pushed the door open and stood back so Brooke could go in ahead of me. "The tenant herself gave him a key."

"Does that mean he's authorized to give it out to anyone he wants?" She went in, and I followed.

"We'll let him be responsible for that."

The entrance way was narrow, with slatted sliding doors on the left. Beyond it, the living room was split vertically by a rude loft, painted white, about seven feet off the ground. The edge of a quilt was visible along one side of it.

I climbed two rungs of a ladder with two-by-four rails and looked over the edge. A full-sized mattress, neatly made, filled most of the space, a small nightstand beside it and a plethora of pillows of all shapes and sizes scattered around.

"It's really kind of nice up here," I said.

Brooke didn't believe me. "Let me see," she said, tugging at my arm and wedging herself onto the ladder beside me. "Not too bad," she conceded.

We stepped down. Only about half of the living room was under the loft, a 25-inch TV set sitting diagonally in the darkest corner. A painted rocker, a floor lamp, and an old sofa with wooden arms sat out in the open. I walked through the living room to the kitchen, passing a tiny bathroom with a rust-stained tub.

In the kitchen, two plates, two glasses, a mug, and two sets of flatware sat on the Rubbermaid drain board. There was no dishwasher. In the cabinets over the sink were a couple more plates, two bowls, three more glasses, and half-a-loaf of bread. Beneath the sink was an open can of Comet and some dish detergent. I opened the refrigerator: A half-gallon of milk, a quart of juice, a bowl of grapes covered with plastic wrap, and two containers of yogurt. There was cheese and some sandwich meat in the meat drawer, a bag of salad in one of the bottom drawers, and a couple of apples in the other.

"Robin, take a look at this."

I closed the refrigerator and left the kitchen. Brooke was in the bathroom looking into the medicine cabinet over the sink. There was a safety razor, a toothbrush, a bottle of ibuprofen, and a can of shaving cream. What caught my eye, though, were the birth control pills. I took down the dispenser and opened it. About a third of the pills were missing, the last empty space under the label for Monday, the day of the murder.

"I'd say she left in a hurry," Brooke said.

I nodded. "She didn't come back here after driving off with my car."

"But when she left her apartment, she didn't expect to be leaving town."

"She's got a record," I said. "She's jumped bail or something. Rodney Burns is going to get a match on those prints."

"Arlington would be his best bet." Brooke pointed to the label. A Walgreens in Arlington, Virginia, had dispensed the Loestrin just over a year ago. The prescribing physician was a Dr. Yarbrough.

"I'll let Rodney know," I said.

Melissa's clothes were behind the slatted doors just inside the front door. She didn't have a lot of them, but those she had were nice.

"This is cute," Brooke said, holding a blouse and a skirt in front of her.

"Wouldn't fit you," I said.

"I wasn't…What do you mean it won't fit me? What are you implying?"

I grinned at her. Brooke was both hippier and bustier than Melissa, but I wasn't going to be the one to say it.

"Melissa?" called a masculine voice. The door pushed inward, and I stepped away from it. A dark-haired guy in his middle twenties looked in at us. He needed both a haircut and a shave, but in spite of that looked good enough to eat.

"Sorry," I said. "Just us chickens."

"I'm Brad," he said. "Where's Melissa?"

"No idea. We expected to find her here."

"How did you get in?"

"Can't you guess?" I asked.

He looked at the deadbolt and the doorframe. He said, "Used a key?"

"Yep."

"She give it to you?"

"Matt did."

Brad nodded. "The boyfriend," he said.

"You haven't seen Melissa recently, have you?" I asked.

"Not for a couple of days."

"Me either," I said. "I'm Robin Starling."

"Brad Flowers," he said.

"Brooke Marshall," Brooke said.

He gave us a slow smile. "I'm very glad to meet you."

"We're worried about her," I said. "She just disappeared without telling anyone where she was going. You don't have any ideas, do you?"

His smile changed, lifting one corner of his mouth. "I have some ideas, but not about where Melissa could be," he said.

I thought maybe there was a double entendre in that somewhere, but I ignored it. "Does she have any family that you know about?"

He lifted his shoulders and dropped them. "She moved in about six months ago. If you bring over a six-pack, she'll sit on the couch with you and help you drink it. That's about all I know."

"Thanks, Brad," I said.

"Listen. We're having a party tomorrow night, just down the hall at the apartment on the end. Both of you are invited, if you want to come."

Brooke smiled at him. "We might just be there," she said.

"Cool. It's at eight o'clock."

When he had gone, I shut the door. "Social life a little slow?" I said.

"We'll see more people from the apartment building. We might find out something about Melissa."

"Good point."

"And meet some really cute guys," Brooke said.

I rolled my eyes.

"Going to call Rodney?"

I nodded, my gaze sweeping over the apartment in search of a phone, which Melissa evidently didn't have.

"I think a cell phone is wasted on you." She fished her own cell from her purse and handed it to me.

"I don't know his number," I said, taking it.

Brooke took the phone back and returned it to her purse.

Chapter 14

I called Rodney Burns when I got back to my office. When I had identified myself, he said, "I haven't got anything yet."

"I got a look at one of Melissa's old medicine bottles, which may tell us where she came from."

He waited.

"Arlington, Virginia," I said.

There was a pause. Maybe he was writing it down. "That may help," he said finally. "I know someone up there I can call." Another pause. "I'll let you know if I find anything."

I had a letter-brief to write for a case in circuit court. The phone rang as I was proofreading it for the third time. I sent the document to the printer as I picked up the phone.

"Robin Starling."

"Robin, it's Brooke."

I turned in my chair to look at the clock on my desk. It was nearly five. "Hey, Brooke."

"I've got Derek's files set up on my computer. If you can bring home a ream of letterhead, we can print out letters to let all the debtors know to keep sending their money."

"Whose letterhead? Mine or Derek's?"

"Well, Derek is dead. I was thinking you could introduce yourself as attorney for the estate…"

"Got it," I said.

"Have you ever thought that the murderer could be somebody who owes Derek money? It gives us 58 more potential suspects."

"Just what we need."

"The debtor comes in to make a payment or to plead for more time, then shoots Derek and takes his note from the drawer. Bingo, the debt's erased."

"But not from the Peachtree file," I said.

"Probably not from the Peachtree file."

"So what you're looking for is a computer record of an outstanding note that doesn't have a corresponding paper copy in those files we took. It's an idea. Could you check it out for me?"

"I'm working on it," she said.

After I hung up, I got a phone book out of the drawer. If I could locate Mark Walker, it would be a good afternoon's work.

But I didn't, and it wasn't. I left the office about 5:00 so I could stop by the Y on my way home. Women crowded the locker room getting ready for an aerobics class, but the basketball gym was empty. I dribbled the ball and shot baskets for a while, waiting for enough people to show up for a pickup game, but no one came.

Eventually, I stood at the free throw line, counting baskets to see how many consecutive shots I could make. It was how I always ended practice when nobody showed up. Sometimes I missed a shot after only half-a-dozen or so, but I often broke twenty, and today I found myself settling into a zone where everything functioned automatically. Shot after shot fell through the hoop without doing more than graze the rim. Rather than have to run down the ball, I stepped forward to recover it, then stepped back to shoot again.

My fiftieth basket got my attention, and I started thinking about what I was doing, a little on my fifty-first shot, a little more on my fifty-second. I missed on basket fifty-six and had to chase down the ball.

There was a guy standing just inside the door watching me. He was good-looking, maybe three or four years younger than I was, but the white T-shirt and white gym shorts that looked like underwear didn't do much for him.

"How many was that?" he asked me.

"Fifty-five."

"In a row? You always do that?"

"Never. I think I once hit forty-nine out of fifty when I was in college."

He nodded. "Cool."

I tossed him the ball and headed down to the locker room to get my clothes. My performance at the free throw line had redeemed what had been a tough day. For nearly thirty minutes, I had not thought about Larsen or my father or the Nolan case. I had not even been aware that such people existed. It was for such moments that I had always devoted so much time to athletics.

* * *

Brooke hadn't turned up a missing note by the time I got home. She was sitting at one of the computers in the bedroom we used as an office.

"I didn't accomplish anything either," I told her. "There's no Mark Walker in the phonebook, and he doesn't seem to be related to any of the Walkers that are."

"Maybe he doesn't have a phone."

"At least no land line. And if he has a cell, I couldn't find it on the Internet." I headed back to my bedroom to hang up my dress and put my shoes in the closet. I did a little stretching, then stepped into the bathroom for a long, hot shower.

I glanced at the clock when I got out. It was still early, but I figured I was in for the night. I pulled on the big T-shirt I slept in over a fresh pair of panties, then went to the kitchen to rustle up some dinner.

Brooke came in and took one of the stools at the counter. "I found three possibilities," she said.

"That was quick." I got out the open bottle of wine in the refrigerator. Brooke nodded when I held it up, so I slipped two glasses off the rack beneath one of the cabinets and set them on the counter.

"One still owes fifteen thousand dollars, one still owes nine, and one owes fifty," she said.

I nodded as I poured. If I had gone in and shot Derek Nolan because I owed him too much money, I wouldn't take just my own note. That would focus attention on me. I'd want to take several.

"Are the three files together in the alphabet?" I asked.

"B, D, and R," Brooke said.

I put the cork back in the bottle and took a sip of my wine. "Were the B and D together in the drawer?"

Mr. R, I thought, might have done the shooting, then grabbed a couple more files from the front of the drawer to cover himself.

"Six in between," Brooke said.

Mr. R still could have taken them, I thought. I got the salad bag and a leftover piece of steak and some raspberry vinaigrette from the refrigerator. "You want some?" I asked her.

She nodded. "Please."

"There was only one bullet in Derek Nolan," I said, voicing my theory. "But one person could have taken the other two files to spread suspicion."

"Or two people came in right behind the murderer, one after the other. When they saw Nolan dead, each got his file and left."

"Or somebody else entirely did the killing and took all three files to divert suspicion," I said.

"Somebody else with a motive unrelated to Derek's loan-shark business."

We kept coming back to my clients. I made a face as I chopped up the steak and put it on the salad. Brooke sat watching me as I sprinkled on the vinaigrette.

"There's another possible explanation for the missing files," she said at last. "One that has nothing to do with the murder."

I divided up the salad and pushed Brooke's plate over to her.

"Maybe Liz Lockard's Peachtree file wasn't up to date," she said as she speared a piece of meat with her fork. "Derek Nolan was a high-interest-rate lender. Maybe three people came up with lower-cost sources of funds and came in to pay him off. He marked the notes paid, returned them to the debtors, and moved the files from his active drawer to the inactive file cabinet."

"And the reason Liz didn't make the changes in her computer…"

"Is because she was out and he didn't tell her."

I nodded and ate some salad. "Or he told her, but she's lazy and never got around to it," I said.

"Or she's lazy," Brooke conceded.

"In either case, the files would be in the lateral file cabinet."

Brooke nodded. "I've got a call in to Matt."

"No answer?"

"No," she said.

"I wonder where he is."

"Maybe he has a night class, or he's at the library studying."

"Maybe he's out looking for his fiancée," I said.

"I doubt he'll find her."

"Always the optimist."

When the doorbell rang, I was curled up in the living room with the latest edition of *Runners' World*.

Brooke went to the door and looked through the peephole. "It's Matt Nolan," she said. I started to get up. Brooke was dressed, but I was wearing a T-shirt that barely covered my panties.

She opened the door. "Hi, Matt."

"Hi, Brooke. I found two of the notes." He held the files up. Catching sight of me, he said, "Hey, Robin."

I sat hastily, holding the magazine on my lap for cover.

"Which ones are they?" I called.

"Bein and Radford."

B and R. That left D as our suspect.

"Come on in," Brooke said. She led him into the living room, evidently oblivious to my state of undress. When she sat beside me on the couch, Matt took the club chair, which put the coffee table between us and provided me at least a little camouflage.

"Yes," Brooke said. "They're two of the missing files." She looked at my long, bare legs and raised an eyebrow. Matt was looking, too, but with both eyebrows up. It occurred to me that I might not be as camouflaged as I thought.

I said, "So that leaves…"

"Dillon," Brooke said. "Michael Dillon. According to Peachtree, he owes fifteen thousand and change. I don't remember exactly."

"It gives us someone to talk to. We can look him up tomorrow."

Matt said, "Won't that be dangerous?"

"He may not be our guy," I said. "This is kind of a long shot."

"But if he is your guy…"

"We'll be careful. Where does he live?"

Brooke opened the file. Matt's head was down, but his gaze cut toward me and away. I looked down. My panties, with their broad stripes in primary colors, were clearly visible through and below the T-shirt.

"Excuse me," I said. I stood up and went around the end of the couch to go back to the bedrooms. I felt as if they were watching me, but I didn't look back. As I reached the hallway, I heard a snort of laughter, I couldn't tell from whom. I looked down and sighed, then twitched the T-shirt down over my fanny.

"House in Carytown," Brooke called. "Grove Avenue."

"Got it," I shouted. In my bedroom, I got a pair of jeans off a hanger in the closet and pulled them on as I hobbled back down the hall to the living room. Matt and Brooke turned around and looked at me as I came in. Neither one of them busted out laughing, so I thought maybe I was decent.

"We can call on him tomorrow," I said. I sat back down on the couch and put my bare feet on the edge of the coffee table. Matt's eyes went to them, and so I put them back on the floor. A guy his age, maybe a woman's bare feet were arousing.

"You know," I said, "we're running down these long-shots because we can't find your fiancée. She's the critical witness in this case. If she were to show up and say the man she saw had hair on his head, or a beard, or was unusually short or something, we'd be in the clear. She didn't tell you anything?"

Matt shook his head. "She just said a man. We all assumed…"

"Yeah, I know. I guess you noticed that she didn't run off until after the police showed up."

He looked startled.

"The police came, she took off in my car, and nobody ever saw her again. She hasn't returned to her apartment and hasn't returned to work. You don't have a theory for why she disappeared?"

"No. None."

"She really intended to marry you, you think."

His smile was more like an expression of pain. "I think," he said.

"She's from northern Virginia?"

"I thought she was from Pennsylvania."

113

"Really? She told you that?"

"I...I'm pretty sure she's from somewhere around Philadelphia. She grew up in one of the suburbs."

"She say which one?"

"I don't remember. Maybe."

"Is it the kind of thing you would remember?"

"Maybe not."

I nodded. Men, I thought. I looked at Brooke, wondering how we were going to get rid of our guest, now that we'd gotten what we could out of him.

"Have you been going to class?" she asked him. "You're still in school, aren't you?"

"Yes, technically. I've been to some of my classes."

"Uh oh," Brooke said.

He shrugged.

"Do you have any classes tomorrow?"

"Yes. I have a nine o'clock."

Brooke looked at her watch. "It's a long way back to your house, and it's getting late. Would you like to crash here on the couch?"

"Yeah. Sure," he said.

I tried not to roll my eyes.

Chapter 15

Matt was still asleep the next morning when I cut through the living room to get my orange juice. The coffeemaker started sputtering while I was pouring, and I knew Brooke wasn't far behind me. I took my juice into the living room, sat, and propped my feet up on the ottoman. I'd pulled on a pair of gym shorts, though Matt's eyes were closed and it didn't really matter. To paraphrase a commercial for a big motel chain, everyone looks fully clothed when you're asleep.

The coffeemaker reached the end of its brewing cycle, and, as its sputtering increased in volume, Brooke came through wearing a long-sleeved, silk pajama-top that came down to mid-thigh. It looked like she'd run a brush through that thick, red hair of hers, which put her one-up on me, though she was scratching her rump sleepily as she went by me, giving only a glance at the sleeping figure on the couch.

Once she'd got her coffee, she came back and sat beside me on the loveseat.

Matt was lying on his back, bare-chested, one arm over the side of the couch and touching the floor. A leg stuck out from under the twisted sheet.

Brooke sipped her coffee. "Do you think he shaves his chest?" she murmured softly.

"Does a bear poop in the woods?"

She looked at me. "What does that mean?"

"He must," I said. "Men's chests aren't completely hairless like that. Maybe Asians' are," I amended. "Native Americans'." I took a swallow of juice.

"He even shaves his pits," Brooke said.

"Evidently. Probably if you got close enough, you'd see he had some stubble."

She didn't move to the couch to check it out. She just sipped her coffee and watched Matt sleep. I sipped my juice and did the same. I didn't feel any particular inclination to move when I'd finished my juice. Watching Matt sleep was proving to be a surprisingly pleasant way to pass the time.

After ten minutes or so, though, Matt snorted explosively and sat up. He looked at us, a little wild-eyed. "What is it?" he said.

"What's what?" I asked.

"What's wrong?"

I exchanged looks with Brooke. She said, "Nothing's wrong, that we know of."

"Then why…" He looked down, flipped the sheet over his bare leg, then swung both feet to the floor. "Why are you just sitting there looking at me?"

I shrugged. "I'm drinking my morning orange juice. You want some? Or there's coffee."

Brooke nodded. Matt looked around the room as if still trying to get his bearings, jerking his head as his gaze shifted.

"I'll get you that coffee," I said, and stood up.

* * *

"So, how'd you like sharing a bathroom with him this morning?" I asked Brooke as she drove us toward Carytown.

"It was okay. He probably wasn't in the shower five minutes."

"I noticed you found him a safety razor. He managed to cut himself."

She nodded. "He had to put back on his old clothes, though. I didn't have anything for him."

I got a mental image of Matt Nolan in a pair of Brooke's panties, and I snorted.

"What?" Brooke asked.

I shook my head. "Grove Avenue," I said, pointing at the sign. "Get off here."

The house had a low-ceilinged porch with square brick pillars. The door was dark wood and beveled glass. I pressed the doorbell, and it jangled deep inside the house. We waited. My watch said eight-fifteen, so it was possible that we had missed him. Having an extra person in the house when you wake up tends to slow you down.

Brooke nudged me, and I looked up, seeing the short, dark-haired man coming toward us just as I heard the sound of his feet on the hardwood floor. There wasn't a rug in the front room of the house. Some nice mahogany furniture, but no rug.

The knocker clacked as he pulled open the door. "Hello," he said. "What can I do for you?" He wore a polo shirt, and his belly spilled over jeans worn low on his hips.

"Michael Dillon?" I said.

"That would be me." From further in the house, I could hear children's voices and the clatter of tableware.

"Sorry to disturb your breakfast," I said. "We wanted to ask you about your loan with Derek Nolan."

He stepped back into the house, which I took as an invitation to come in. I nodded Brooke ahead of me and crowded behind her. Michael Dillon went and stood by a wingchair, but didn't sit. "What about the loan?" he said.

"It was for fifteen thousand dollars?"

"Twenty, originally. I think I got it down to fifteen or so before I went in and paid it off."

"When was that?"

He shrugged. "Couple of weeks ago maybe. Jen?" he called.

A heavily freckled woman with straight brown hair appeared in the door of the kitchen.

"When did I go in to pay off Derek Nolan?" Michael asked.

"Four weeks ago tomorrow," she said. "Catherine, put that down." Something thudded, a child screamed, and Jen disappeared back into the kitchen.

Michael shrugged at us. "Time flies," he said.

"Derek Nolan was murdered earlier this week," I said.

"I heard that."

"And he doesn't seem to have left any documentation of that final payment. I'm hoping you have a copy of the note or something."

"Are you Mrs. Nolan?" he asked.

"I'm a lawyer representing the estate."

His gaze cut to Brooke.

"My sidekick," I said. "You can call her Tonto."

It surprised a burst of laughter from him. "Just a minute. I'll see if I can find it."

He went into the kitchen. I could make out his voice and Jen's amid the sound of childish voices and laughter. After a few minutes, he came out again with a manila folder.

"How many kids do you have back there?" Brooke asked him.

He smiled a little ruefully. "Only four," he said.

"Only!"

"Sometimes it seems like quite enough." He opened the file and handed me the paper on top. "That what you're looking for?"

What he handed me was a promissory note, marked paid and signed by Mark Walker for Derek Nolan.

"I don't guess you have a copy machine here," I said.

"As a matter of fact, I do. You know, it's interesting. This isn't the first time I've been asked to produce a copy of this."

"Really?"

"A couple of weeks or so ago I ran into Derek Nolan at the Commonwealth Club. My in-laws are members there, so Jen and I get to go have dinner sometimes. He seemed surprised to hear I'd paid this off. Decided he had a few glitches in his filing system."

Michael Dillon disappeared back into the house with the file. I looked at Brooke, and she raised her eyebrows. He seemed an unlikely murderer. On the other hand, it seemed we had found the subject of Mark Walker's alleged embezzlement.

Chapter 16

Brooke dropped me off in front of the office building, and I took the elevator up. "I'm here," I told the receptionist. "Call Pete." I gave her a smile.

Jennifer looked flustered. "I'm sorry," she said. "Mr. Larsen…He told me he wanted to see you as soon as you got in."

I waved a hand in forgiveness. "It's all right. Do you mean he wants to see me today?"

"No. That was yesterday. There is a Mr. Burns here to see you, though."

I turned my head and saw him, getting up from a chair, his scalp shining through his thinning hair. He'd changed suits—this one was a solid blue—but it looked just as rumpled as the brown one had. Maybe he had given up on clothes hangers and kept his suits in a jumble on his closet floor.

"Mr. Burns," I said.

"Ms. Starling." He nodded his head at me. "I think I've found your girl."

"Come on back." I led him down the hall to my office.

"Tell me about her," I said, pointing him to a client chair and walking around my desk.

"Her real name is Melanie Burke."

"M.B." I sat and pulled over a yellow legal pad.

"Yes. She kept the same initials when she moved to Richmond." He opened his attaché case and took out a three-page memo, stapled at the corner. I put down my pen.

"I wouldn't have said she looked like a Melanie," I said, irrelevantly.

"She was out on bail for criminal assault when the victim died. The charge changed to murder, but before they could pick her up, she disappeared."

"How long ago?"

"Nine months. The Arlington police would really like to find her."

"Join the club."

Burns said, "She got into an altercation with her boyfriend, evidently. They lived in one of the older high-rise apartment buildings off I-95. He dangled her off the eighteenth-floor balcony and threatened to drop her."

I snorted incredulously.

"According to witnesses, hung her over the rail so that her knees on the bar and his grip on her ankles were all that was keeping her from falling. He was moving her feet up and down and laughing like a crazy man, and she was screaming profanity at him. It seemed to have attracted half the neighbors in the building before he tired of it and pulled her back in."

"And when she got back inside she assaulted him," I said.

"Yes."

"Stabbed him?"

"Actually, she hit him in the head with a baseball bat and castrated him with a steak knife."

I cringed, but Burns continued tonelessly, "Evidently, he was high on ecstasy at the time, so it's possible he didn't even know it was happening."

I didn't say anything.

"Ms. Starling?"

I shook myself. "I'm sorry. I'm waiting for my flesh to stop crawling."

He nodded.

"This doesn't get us any closer to finding her, does it?" I said.

"Probably not. It does tell you why she disappeared again when she found herself at a murder scene with police on the way."

"How did you know about that?"

He smiled thinly. "Your associate gave me some background when she called to set up your appointment. I got a few more details from the newspaper, and a secretary in the police department is a special friend of mine."

I raised my eyebrows, wondering what kind of friend a "special friend" was.

"She faxed me the statement of a Matthew Nolan."

I nodded.

He took an envelope from the inside pocket of his jacket. "I have my bill here. I don't know how you want to handle it."

I didn't know how I wanted to handle it either, but I took the envelope and opened it. The bill was for 650 dollars. I nodded. "Seems reasonable," I said, and dropped it on my desk. I had a couple of problems to resolve before I could pay it. I hadn't arranged for my clients to pay me yet, and of course Larsen had told me to drop the case.

"There's one more thing you could do for me," I said.

Burns raised his eyebrows.

"I'm trying to locate a Mark Walker."

He took a small yellow pad from the same jacket pocket from which he had extracted his bill. "Tell me what you know about him," he said.

I told him.

"It shouldn't be too hard," he said when I was done.

"I'm glad to hear it."

Chapter 17

By five o'clock, I hadn't managed to get anything else done on the Bruno-Nolan case. As routine as preliminary hearings generally were, this was only the second of my career, and I needed to spend time preparing for it. Though it was Friday, I packed some of the files in my briefcase before heading down to my car.

I had entered the parking garage before I remembered that my car wasn't there. Brooke had driven me to work that morning. I fished my cell phone out of my purse and hit "3" on the speed dial. After four rings, I got shunted to her voicemail. I frowned and closed the phone.

I went back into the office building. Standing in the lobby, I looked out at the street. Headlights were on in the early dusk of late October. No parking was permitted along the street during rush hour, and I knew Brooke couldn't be waiting at the curb for me to come out, but I pushed through the revolving door to look.

A river of headlights flowed toward me and past me. From where I stood, I could see, several blocks away, the corner of the hotel where Lynn had gone to meet Steve Bruno. I looked back up the one-way street in the direction Brooke would be coming from, hoping that she would slide to a stop against the curb as I stood there.

After a couple of minutes, I said, "Well, crap." I went back inside and took the elevator up to my floor. Just down from my office, a light was on. It was John Parker, working late.

I walked past my office and looked in on him. He was on his feet behind his desk, shoving files into an accordion-style briefcase.

"No hot date?" I said from the doorway.

He jumped, then shook his head as he closed the briefcase and clicked the tongue into place. "Not tonight. Not unless you're volunteering."

I made a face. "I find myself stranded," I said.

"You need a ride?"

"Were you going home from here?"

"Yeah, sure." He got his jacket from the hanger on the back of his door and shrugged into it. "Let's go."

We rode down the elevators without talking. John and I lived only a couple of miles apart in the West End. While we had been dating, we carpooled together more often than not. After he cheated on me, that stopped, along with a number of other things that it would make me blush to tell you about.

In the parking garage, John and I put our briefcases in the floor of the back seat on opposite sides of the car, then got in the front. As he backed out of his space, one hand braced on my headrest, John said, "What happened?"

"What do you mean?"

"In normal circumstances, you'd rather walk home than catch a ride with me. What's up?"

"It would be more accurate to say I'd rather drive myself than catch a ride with you," I said. "Brooke was supposed to pick me up, but she didn't show and I can't get her on her cell."

"So riding with me ranks above walking home." He put the car in drive and started winding his way down out of the garage. "It's something," he said.

I nodded. "High praise," I agreed. "It might surprise you to learn that having dinner with you ranks above eating out of trashcans."

"Whoa," he said, braking to a stop at the garage exit. "You're going to have me panting." After he'd pulled into traffic, he glanced at me. "That wasn't a hint, was it? You're not inviting yourself out to dinner."

"No, I'm not."

"I didn't think so. Doesn't hurt to check."

"Oh, don't act so woebegone! You're not interested in me."

"How can you say that?"

"Let me rephrase: You're not more interested in me than any other piece of tail."

He accelerated onto the Downtown Expressway, his fingers picking change for the toll out of his center console. He closed the console with his elbow. "One indiscretion and that's it, isn't it? I'm forever branded as a philandering creep."

"That's like Lynn Nolan bending over her husband's cooling body and saying, 'Why can't you forgive me Derek? It was just one murder.'"

His eyes cut toward me as he lowered his window, but he had to look away again to chuck his change into the toll bin. The light changed from red to green, and he accelerated. "You think she did it then?" Ahead of us were two streams of taillights as far as I could see.

"No. At least I hope she didn't. I was just making a point."

"Yeah, I got the point. You're still handling the case?"

"I am. What do you know about it?"

"The word is Larsen pulled you off it."

"He can't actually pull me off it. I'm attorney of record. It's going to take a judge to cut me loose, and in the meantime the preliminary hearing's Tuesday."

John shook his head. "You're a law unto yourself," he said. "You just do whatever the hell you want to do."

"Not all the time."

"All the time. You're a good person, but you're chaotic good."

"What? What's chaotic good?"

"It's an old Dungeons-and-Dragons term."

"You played Dungeons and Dragons?"

He moved his head uncomfortably. "In high school."

"I can't picture it. Did you wear a pocket protector and go around with an H-P calculator dangling from your belt?"

He looked irritated. "No, and I didn't wear short-sleeve dress shirts and Coke-bottle glasses with thick plastic frames."

"Did you participate in bizarre rituals in sewage drains?"

"None of those either."

I nodded silently, feeling disappointed. The D&D study-geek would have been a fascinating predecessor to someone like John, but the mental image I had conjured was quickly fading, dissipating like so much smoke.

We were on I-64, heading west, when John said, "You know he's going to can you."

"Larsen?"

"He doesn't like seeing his associate attorneys written up in the Times-Dispatch. And he'll only tolerate so much insubordination."

"I guess I've given him a bit to tolerate. Of course, a lot of it's been your fault."

"My fault!"

I looked at him.

"Well, okay. Your last case was maybe my fault. That'll make me feel even worse to see you out of a job." He swung the car onto the exit ramp. As he braked for the light, I leaned across the car to kiss his cheek.

"What was that for?" he said, glancing at me.

"You're concerned about me. That's sweet."

"Unh huh," he said.

When he stopped in front of my house, I thanked him, got out, and waved good-bye to him from the end of my sidewalk. Lights were on in the house. I fished in my purse for my keys as I approached it and didn't realize I was missing them until I got to the porch. Since Melissa Butler had run off with my full set, I'd been operating off three different key rings.

"Rats," I said, realizing that I needed to take time to consolidate those key rings. "Big, long-haired, flea-covered rats." I looked after John, but he was already making the turn at the end of the block. I rang the bell, thinking Brooke might be back from wherever she had gone, but got no answer. I rang again, and something crashed in the interior of the house.

My eyes cut toward the plate glass window to one side of the porch. The window wasn't curtained, but the lawn sloped away from the house, and from outside the hedge I wouldn't be able to see anything other than the living room ceiling. Though I wasn't dressed for it, I stepped down off the stoop and pushed my way between the bushes and the house. Sharp twigs poked against my bottom through my silk dress as I stood on tiptoe to look through the window.

Mine is a big, square living room with a few large, comfortable pieces of furniture set well in from the walls. The floor lamps were off, but enough light came from the kitchen on the right and the hallway on the left to give the living room furniture a strange, half-lit quality. I couldn't see Brooke or anyone else, though. Dropping back onto my heels, I glanced at the front door.

A sound like the bang of a door came from the back of the house. I listened, my heart pounding, but there was only silence.

I rammed my way out through the hedge, heedless of the branches clutching at my dress and raking my skin, and I staggered out onto the lawn. It took a couple of steps to regain my balance, and then I headed around the house at a trot.

A chain-link fence stopped me at the corner. Beyond it, the backyard was darker than the night, shadowed by pine trees. I thought I saw a man moving in the graveled alley, maybe two men. They were shadows among shadows, though, and I could not be sure.

"Hey," I shouted.

For a moment the shadows stopped, then they were moving again, away from me.

I looked for the gate, using my hands as much as my eyes, and when I found it yanked at the handle. My dress caught on something as I went through, but I pulled away, losing one of my pumps in the soft grass and kicking away the other. Almost immediately, I stepped on a pinecone and yelled something that was both unladylike and unprofessional. As I limped across the yard, an engine roared to life. Tires spun against the hard-packed gravel in the alley behind my house. A vehicle jerked into motion—a pickup of some kind. I reached the alley and saw its brake lights flare, but then it turned out of the alley and was gone.

As I turned back toward the house, I felt a breath of air against my side. I put my hand to it and felt a rent in my dress big enough to put my hand through. "Good grief," I said. I started picking my way back across the backyard toward the gate I had come through, but stopped when I noticed some pine-filtered moonlight reflecting unevenly in the panes of the French doors.

I limped toward them and pushed at the partially open door. It swung open with the gentlest of sighs. As I entered the living room, goose bumps breaking out all over my body, I could see through the house to the front door, which was now standing open.

"Son of a gun," I said, wondering how many of them there had been and how many directions they had gone. I walked through the house, looking warily about me, and stepped out onto the front stoop.

A pickup, one of the big ones, slowed to a stop several houses down from me. I had no idea whether it was the one I had seen in the alley. Surely not, but the streetlight was between us, and the night was too dark to make out the color even now.

I walked down the sidewalk, moving closer to the pickup without moving directly toward it. When I was halfway to the street, the license plate, a gray smear of shadow against the front bumper, was almost legible. The tires turned toward me, scratching grittily on the pavement, and I stopped. The engine rumbled powerfully, but the pickup didn't move. It had Virginia plates. The first letter was either an M or a W; in another step I would know which.

My left foot started to rise, but my weight came back down on it when the volume of the pickup's engine leaped upward and the pickup itself lurched into motion, its front-end rising as it surged over the curb toward me. My eyes flicked up to the windshield, but the pickup was moving and the streetlight reflected in the glass, obscuring the cab's interior.

I turned and ran barefoot toward the house, aware already that I couldn't make it. An instant before the truck hit me, I threw myself to the side, the edge of the pickup's bumper just grazing the heel of my foot and sending me spinning. The pickup climbed the steps toward my front door, taking out one of the pillars supporting the gable over the stoop before coming to a stop. I lay looking up at it for an instant, half stunned and breathing hard.

The pickup's reverse lights came on, and its rear tires spat turf as it bounced down off the steps. It skidded to a stop perhaps ten yards from me and came at me again. I staggered up, clutching my right elbow against my side without being aware of any pain. I didn't actually feel anything, physical or emotional. Pain, outrage, panic—all of it was there, somewhere, but it was closed off in a part of my brain where it couldn't distract me. The roar of the engine grew as the truck bore down on me.

This time I didn't have time to get out of the way. I leaped upward, trying to get above the bumper and the front grill. I twisted in the air, drawing my feet up after me, and hit the windshield lengthwise. As I rolled up on top of the cab, a woman screamed—me maybe. Someone was coming across the street. The pickup was still gathering speed, and, as it went over the curb into the road, I bounced off the top of the cab into the bed of the truck, landing in a heap. The truck lurched to a stop, throwing me against the cab, then it took off again, just as I was sitting up, holding to one side of the pickup with my left hand and forearm. Brooke Marshall and Dr. McDermott, the retired physician who lived across the street from me, were standing in the road. I only caught a glimpse of them before the pickup, jerking from one curb to the other as it accelerated, threw me against the far wall of the pickup bed amid a jumble of crumpled beer cans and other detritus.

The back window of the cab was tinted and in the dark completely opaque to me. Though the street curved sharply as it went downhill, the pickup maintained its speed, its suspension squealing. I managed to work my way into a crouch, holding on to the tailgate with one hand and the side of the pickup with the other, but I almost went down when the street came to a T and the pickup went through the stop sign without slowing down, its tires skidding as the rear of the truck slewed sideways.

Nothing, it seemed, was going to slow it down. As the pickup accelerated through another stop sign, I felt the first surge of panic breaking out of whatever closet my brain had consigned it to. There was a traffic light ahead, its light green, as if that mattered, and the pickup swung into the middle of the road as we rocketed toward it. The driver turned hard to the right, starting the turn early, and the truck screeched as if it were coming apart, the tires sliding on the pavement, then losing their grip entirely as the truck went into a spin. It bumped over a curb onto somebody's lawn, bouncing me into the air. I came down on my kiester, bounced, then scrambled over the side, sliding down the rear panel and landing heavily on my back in the grass as the driver regained control of the pickup and bounced over the curb back into the road.

Chapter 18

For a moment I lay stunned, unable to draw a breath, then my diaphragm came unstuck, and my chest rose as my lungs inflated. Lifting my head, I saw that the pickup had stopped a house or two down from me. I lurched to my feet and limped onto the front stoop of a small brick house. I rang the bell, my head turned so as not to lose sight of the pickup. The taillights dimmed as the truck began to roll forward, picking up speed, then the truck from hell was gone.

The porch light came on above my head, and I turned toward the door to give the peephole a shrug and a sick smile. The door swung open. The man inside was significantly taller than I was, wearing a thin cotton bathrobe that didn't quite reach his knees. I looked up into a wide, toothy grin.

"Hello," he said, blinking at me over the unnatural smile.

"I'm sorry to disturb you," I said, and stopped, unnerved by the quaver in my voice.

"It's quite all right." He spoke in a flat, West Texas sort of drawl: *Quat all rat.* At first glance, I had taken him for my own age, about thirty, but the web

135

of seams about his eyes and mouth suggested that I had misjudged him by maybe twenty years.

"Thank you," I said. "I…" I had thought to give some explanation for my appearance on his doorstep, but suddenly it all seemed too complex and unbelievable. "I don't know," I said. I looked down and realized that half my dress had been torn away and my bra was showing. I pulled at the edges of what remained of the silk in an effort to cover myself, but the material didn't seem to be there, and the left cone of my bra continued to shine at the man like a headlight.

It was all too much, and I began to cry. I was ashamed of myself for doing it. It was more of an imposition than coming up to the man's house and shining my breast at him, but I didn't seem to be able to help myself. "I'm sorry," I said. "It's just been so…" You shouldn't try to cry and talk at the same time. My chest hitched, and a line of snot squirted out of my right nostril onto my upper lip. It checked my crying in mid-sob; then, mortified, I began to cry harder.

My host had taken a step backwards, his smile dimming, but his lips never closing completely over his slightly protruding teeth. His hands rose in front of his chest, his palms turned out defensively as he cringed away from me. I felt bad for him, and, reaching out, I laid a hand on his arm.

"I'm sorry about this," I said, sniffing, trying to get myself under control. "I know it's just awful."

He nodded, reaching behind himself with one hand and groping on the spindle-legged secretary in his little entranceway. He found what he was looking for, a box of facial tissues, and he thrust it at me protectively. "Kleenex?" he said.

"Thank you." I took several, held them to my face, and snorted.

He waited, still leaning slightly away from me, as if to see if the Kleenex would appease me.

I wiped my nose, folded over the tissues and dabbed at my eyes. I smiled at him, and he seemed to relax a little. "I'm not normally like this," I said, as if he were contemplating a relationship with me and he cared what I was normally like.

"No, I'm sure you're not." He tried out his smile on me again, and this time the smile seemed not unnatural, but only defensive.

I looked around for some place to put my spent tissues, but I didn't see a trashcan. He held out his hand. I hesitated, looking up into his face.

"I'll take them." *Al take them.*

I gave him a half-shrug and a lopsided smile, then folded the tissues over again and handed them to him. His hand closed on them, but he remained where he was, his eyes on my face.

"I guess I need to use your phone," I said.

"What happened?"

"I don't know. Someone broke into my house, I think. They..." I stopped. *They tried to kill me* sounded too dramatic.

He was nodding as if he understood. "Where do you live?" he asked.

I opened my mouth and found that for a moment I couldn't remember my own address. "Beechnut Street," I said finally.

He nodded, and his Adam's apple bobbed in his neck. "My name's Ralph Mitchell," he said.

"I'm sorry. Robin Starling." I held out my hand. He shifted the wad of tissues to his left, and we shook.

"The phone's by the bed. Back there." He jerked his head in the direction of the hall. At the end of it, a fan of light spilled from one of the rooms.

I nodded, hesitated, then moved past him.

The bed was covered by a white chintz spread, thrown back, and a table lamp was on. A library copy of *Barnaby Rudge*, Charles Dickens' fourth or fifth novel—I know because I was an English major—lay open, face down, on the spread.

The telephone was on the nightstand by the table lamp and another box of Kleenex. It was a heavy, black phone with a rotary dial. I had last seen one at my grandma's house when I was a very little girl. I put it on my lap and dialed my home number.

Click-click-click-click-click-click. Click-click. Click-click-click-click. Eventually, I had it dialed.

Brooke answered. "Hello?"

"Where have you been?" I asked.

"Thank heavens you're okay."

"Relatively speaking," I said. "Is everything all right there?"

"Someone broke into our house," she said. "Are you really okay?"

"Yeah. A little scratched and bruised." Looking down at myself, I could have added *half-undressed*, but I didn't. "Do you know what they were after?"

"I think they were after me," Brooke said.

"You? Why would they be after you?"

"I don't know. They kept talking about a redhead."

"You heard this from across the street?"

"No. I heard that from under my bed while two sets of feet stomped around my room."

I didn't have anything to say to that.

"Dr. McDermott is here with me. Where are you?"

I looked up. Ralph Mitchell was looming in the doorway, angular and awkward-seeming, even in his own house. "I don't know. At a house a mile or so away, I think."

"It's 922 Hilliard Street," Ralph said.

"922 Hilliard," I repeated.

"Do you need us to come get you?"

"That would be nice. I've lost my shoes, and I'm not really in any condition to walk it."

"I'll drive you," Ralph said from the doorway, "if you need a ride."

"We'll see you soon," Brooke said.

"Thanks." When I hung up, I looked up at Ralph. "They're coming to get me. I've already ruined your evening." I pointed at his book. "I'm sorry."

"Can I lend you a T-shirt?"

I looked down at myself, then up again. I smiled at him crookedly. "You're a champ," I said.

We waited in the living room, Ralph seated on the sofa and me in a wingchair set at right angles to it. Glancing at him, I wondered what he did for a living—or whether he stayed in his house, reading library books and living off a small inheritance his mother had left him. The newest thing I'd seen in his house was the T-shirt I was wearing, a crisply folded, unfaded shirt bearing the Washington Nationals logo.

My grandma had been like that: she would never wear anything new until she was sure she had gotten all the use there was to get out of the old one. The slippers she wore got so ratty, every Christmas people gave her two or three new pairs. She'd put the new slippers in her closet against the day when her old ones wore out, and she'd died still wearing the old ones, with six new pairs of slippers lined up neatly in her closet. Of course, Grandma had grown up during the Great Depression. I didn't know what Ralph's excuse was.

In front of the house a car door slammed, and Ralph said, "Here they are." He was still grinning, but the smile looked forced, ill at ease.

I reached toward him and patted his hand, which rested on his knee. "Thanks, Ralph. You've been great."

He nodded.

"I'll get this laundered and get it back to you as soon as I can."

He shook his head. "I have plenty of T-shirts."

I was willing to bet this was his only new one. He stood up, and, impulsively, I put my arms around him and gave him a hug.

"Thanks again," I said.

He nodded, looking a little flushed and still grinning helplessly at me.

I went to the door. When I looked back from the end of the sidewalk, he was standing in the doorway. I felt a pang as I raised a hand to wave at him.

He held up his own hand in response, but he didn't wave it. He just stood there on his porch, looking forlorn despite his grin, like an abandoned child.

As we pulled away, Brooke said, "Who was that?"

"Ralph Mitchell." I was sitting in the back seat, and she was sitting in the front, turned sideways with her arm hooked over the back of the seat.

Dr. McDermott, behind the wheel of the big Town Car, said, "Where do you know him from?"

"I don't. The pickup just happened to be driving by his house when I jumped out of it."

Dr. McDermott nodded as he drove, bent over the steering wheel.

"Tell me what happened," I said to Brooke.

"You first."

"There's not much to tell. You didn't show up at work to pick me up…"

"I was waiting for you to call."

"Ah. By the time I thought of that, it was late, and you weren't answering."

"I was probably under the bed by that time."

"That's what I want to hear about."

"I want to hear why you're wearing a Washington Nationals T-shirt."

I lifted the shirt so she could see the condition of my dress underneath.

"Oh," she said. Dr. McDermott's eyes were watching me in the rearview mirror. I lowered the shirt, and the car jolted to a stop as his eyes returned to the road and he saw the stop sign.

"Sorry," he said. "I'm seventy-five years old. It's not every day a pretty girl shows me her underwear."

"I forgot my keys," I said. "I waded into the bushes to look through the front window, then, when I heard one of the French doors slam, went around to the back of the house. I came back through and a pickup tried to run me over in the street."

"We saw that," Brooke said.

"Why did you jump on top of the pickup?" Dr. McDermott asked.

"I didn't have time to get out of the way."

"It was a terrific display of gymnastic ability."

"I muffed the landing. It hurt like hell."

Dr. McDermott gave a dry, wheezy laugh. I made a face at him in the rearview mirror, but he was making a turn and didn't see it.

"So what happened to you?" I asked Brooke. "How did they get in?"

"Someone rang the bell. I went and looked, and nobody was there."

"So you opened the door," I said.

"No, I didn't open the door. Do you think I'm an idiot?"

Actually, I was thinking it was what I might have done.

"Nobody was there, and nobody answered when I called out, so I turned the thumblatch to lock the deadbolt and went back to my room. On the way back, I snatched up the telephone."

"So what happened?"

"They came in the French doors."

"Broke in?"

"Walked in. It was a nice afternoon, and I'd been on the patio getting a little sun on my legs. I guess I forgot to lock the doors when I came in."

She was a redhead and shouldn't be getting any sun on her legs, but we'd had that conversation before.

"I heard them coming in and scooted under my bed before they got to my bedroom."

"Who were they?"

"I don't know. Two people wearing flared jeans and sneakers. Little Feet was wearing Reeboks. Big Feet's had a logo I didn't recognize. He had a pronounced southern drawl, but he spoke softly and most of the time I couldn't even make out what he was saying. Little Feet had a big, foghorn sort of voice."

"What was Little Feet saying?"

"They wanted us for something. They didn't say what."

"Both of us?"

"They didn't call either of us by name. It was Red, or the redhead, and that lawyer bitch."

"That would be me," I said.

McDermott turned onto Beechnut and slowed as we saw two patrol cars parked in front of my house.

"Great," I said drily.

"No, this is good," Dr. McDermott said. "You've got to report this."

I sighed.

"Anyway," Brooke said, "the doorbell rang again while I was under the bed. I thought it might be you. When they went into the living room, I slid out from under. I was afraid you'd come right through the door and walk into them."

"I would have, if I hadn't forgotten my keys."

"I picked a candle up off the nightstand, the one in the heavy round base, and heaved it down the hall into your bedroom. I think I broke a lamp."

"I heard that."

"It spooked the intruders, evidently. They ran back to your bedroom, then they ran out again. When I heard them go out the back door, I went out the front."

McDermott said, "She ran across to my house and got me." He parked in front of his house, across from the patrol cars, and opened the door to get out.

Brooke said, "We didn't even notice the pickup until it charged up onto the lawn to get you."

"Well, I don't guess there's any way to find it now," I said. "I couldn't even tell you whether it was a Ford or a Dodge."

"I saw the license plate," McDermott said.

We both looked at him. "Do you remember the number?" I asked.

"I'm old," he said. "I'm not senile."

Chapter 19

The next day, Saturday, a Sergeant Stebbins called me to say they had run the license plate.

"Who does it belong to?" I asked.

"Mark Walker. Name mean anything to you?"

"It could."

"What's that supposed to mean?"

"It's a common name. A Mark Walker used to work for Derek Nolan, who was murdered last week."

"What do you know about that?"

"I'm the lawyer representing the accused. What does this Mark Walker have to say for himself?"

"He reported his truck stolen at eleven-thirty last night."

"He reported it at eleven-thirty, or it was stolen at eleven-thirty?"

"Reported it. He didn't know when it was stolen, said he last saw it around four yesterday afternoon."

"That's convenient. Have you recovered it, or is it still missing?"

"We've got it. We found it in the parking lot of a grocery store a couple of miles from his house."

I thought about that. "Where is that? Where does he live?"

"Duplex on China Street in Oregon Hill. What I need to know is whether there's any point in bringing him in for a line-up. Would you recognize the driver if you saw him again?"

"I never saw him the first time. Let me check with my roommate." I put my hand over the receiver. "Brooke. They found the owner of the truck, but he reported it stolen last night. Could you pick the burglar out of a lineup?"

She looked up from painting her toenails. "I could pick out his shoes."

"Great." Into the phone I said, "She only saw his feet. There were two of them."

"Two feet?" Stebbins said. "Now that's going to narrow it down."

"Two sets of feet. A pair of little feet wearing Reeboks, and a pair of big feet wearing shoes with a logo she didn't recognize."

Stebbins was silent.

"Does Walker have big feet?"

"Probably. He's six-three or so and weighs around two-forty."

"That matches the description of the Mark Walker I know. Did he have a lot of hair?"

"Not on top. Why?"

"I think that's him. Did you notice what kind of shoes he was wearing?"

"Hell no. Topsiders, I think. Some kind of leather shoe."

"He might have changed shoes."

"Thanks for the tip," Stebbins said.

When I had hung up, I repeated the conversation to Brooke. She was so excited she capped her nail polish and set it aside.

"That's him," she said. "Derek Nolan's collector. Call them back and get them to pick him up."

"Let's think for a minute. Suppose Matt identifies him, and he did used to work for Derek Nolan. What have we got?"

"We've got a man whom Derek Nolan fired trying to run down the lawyer who's representing his wife."

I nodded. "If Walker wasn't driving that truck, it's a heck of a coincidence. Who was with him, do you think?"

She hesitated. "Liz?"

"Liz Lockard? I'd been thinking Little Feet was a man."

"So had I. Liz has that deep carrying voice, though."

"Huh." After a moment, I added, "Let's say it was her. Walker and Lockard broke into our house. What did they want?"

"To kill that bitch of a lawyer, for one thing."

"Well, yes, they tried that. What did they want with you?"

"I don't know. Maybe they wanted to kill me, too."

"It doesn't make any sense."

"No," Brooke agreed. "It would make more sense if they just wanted to kill you."

I made a face at her as I picked up the phone. "I'm going to call Sergeant Stebbins back," I said. "Walker is our guy."

Stebbins, though, was no longer available. I left a message.

"He stepped out," I said, hanging up. "I'm going running. If he calls back, tell him we want to prosecute."

"Be careful out there. It's open season on lawyer-bitches."

"I'll keep that in mind."

Chapter 20

Rodney Burns called on Monday with Mark Walker's address and phone number. "I don't think it will do you any good, though," he said. "He's not at home. There's a warrant out for his arrest on a charge of attempted homicide."

"Ah," I said.

"The victim was one Robin Starling. Would that be you?"

"Unfortunately."

"Rather a coincidence," he said.

"It is."

"Do you want anything else, or should I send you my bill?"

I sighed. "Send the bill, I guess. I can't think of anything else."

I hung up, and almost immediately Sergeant Stebbins called. What he told me I already knew—and, regrettably, had paid money to find out.

"You can't find him?" I asked Stebbins.

"No. We can't."

"Are you looking?"

"We are. We'll let you know when we pick him up."

* * *

I worked late, preparing for the preliminary hearing for Lynn Nolan and Steve Bruno. It seemed to me that the whole thing was hopeless, but I didn't want to go home until I had some kind of a plan. My mother called late in the afternoon. After a moment's hesitation, I picked up.

"Robin!"

"Hi, Mom."

"When are you coming to see me?" Mom lived in Tazewell in western Virginia, which was several hours drive from Richmond.

"I'll be there for Thanksgiving," I said.

"I understand your father came to see you."

Mom was always one to get to the point. "Yeah," I said. "He was here."

"And you threw him out."

"I did not throw him out. How could I have? I didn't even have him thrown out."

"You didn't want to talk to him."

"It's been fifteen years," I said. "What do we have to talk about? Twice a year I get a present from him and a Hallmark card."

"He's been through a lot, you know."

"So have we all."

"It's time to forgive him, Robin. For your sake, if not for his."

It wasn't what I wanted to hear. "You've forgiven him, I take it?"

"I've come to terms with him."

"What does that mean? It sounds like you've signed a contract."

"No. I have forgiven him, I think."

There was a silence.

"You're not saying he's going to be there at Thanksgiving, are you?" I asked.

"Would you come if he was?"

"So he is going to be there."

"We haven't discussed it."

That wasn't an answer, but I let it go. We talked a bit about what my brother was doing—he had a medical practice there in Tazewell — and then ended the call without returning to the subject of Dad.

The rest of the afternoon, my thoughts went to Dad whenever my focus on work relaxed. For a couple of years I'd worked for him summers and after school. Before he moved out on us, I had fully expected to become a veterinarian and join him in the business.

I tried not to think about it. When my phone rang at just after six, I glanced at the phone and saw NAME NOT FOUND in the display window.

Dad, I thought, following up on Mom's call after she had softened me up. I sighed and picked up.

"Hello?"

"Is this Robin Starling?" It was a man's voice, but one with a strong Southern accent. Not the one I'd expected.

"Yes," I said. "Who is this?"

"Mark Walker."

I didn't say anything.

"Does the name mean anything to you?" the voice asked. It was almost too soft to make out over the traffic noises in the background.

"Your truck tried to run me down Friday night," I said.

"I need to talk to you," he said.

"So talk."

"Not on the phone. In person."

"Have you ever seen me? You know what I look like?"

"Not really. I know you're tall."

"So you have seen me."

His breathing was audible. "A glimpse," he said.

"And did I look that stupid?"

"What?"

"I don't know whether it was you who tried to kill me or not, but I have to regard it as a substantial probability. I'm not going to give you a second shot at it."

"They're some things I've got to get off my chest, and you need to hear them," he said.

"For my benefit or yours?" I asked.

"For your clients' benefit. We can meet in a public place. I'm not asking you to meet me in a dark alley or anything."

"How about my office?"

"No. That won't work."

"Where do you suggest?"

"How about the bar of the Tobacco Company?"

It was only a couple of blocks away from me. "When?" I asked.

"Fifteen minutes."

I thought about it. The danger would be getting there, getting in, and getting out again. "Can you give me some idea of what this is about?" I said.

"Not on the phone. I can help you, I think, but I'm going to need some help from you in exchange."

"What kind of help?"

"I'll tell you when I see you."

"Now listen…"

But he had hung up.

"Crap," I said, and dropped the receiver back into its cradle.

I wasn't sure what to do. Certainly, my case needed help—all it could get. On the other hand, I didn't want to put myself within arm's reach of a two-hundred-forty-pound behemoth who wanted to kill me.

Fishing my cell phone from my purse, I held down the "3" key to speed-dial Brooke's cell phone.

"Hi, Robin," she said when she picked up.

"Where are you?"

"At home."

"I just got a call from Mark Walker."

"You're kidding."

"I wish. He wants me to meet him at the Tobacco Company. Says he has something important to tell me that can help in my defense of Lynn and Steve. He won't say what."

"Call the police and let them pick him up. Don't meet him."

"I need to hear what he has to say."

"You don't need to. You don't know he can help your clients; all you know is he says he can. You have every reason to doubt him."

After a moment's hesitation, I said, "I'm going to do it."

"That's crazy."

"At least you know where I am."

"You mean, I'll know where you were headed when you disappeared."

"I'll be careful."

"Trust me, Robin. This is not something you want to do."

"You mean it's not something I should do."

"That's what I said."

"No, you said 'want to do.' What I want is to look Mark Walker in the eyeball and hear what he has to say."

"Wait for me. I'll go with you."

"Can't. He gave me fifteen minutes."

"It's a trap, Robin."

"He sounded sincere."

"Listen to yourself. Anyone can sound sincere."

"It's a public place."

"At least stay on the line," she said. "Tuck your phone out of sight, but leave it on."

"It'll have to be in my purse," I said. "I'm not wearing pockets."

"I may not be able to hear anything."

"I'll shout if I need you. You can call 9-1-1."

Chapter 21

When I emerged from the office building, I found it was twilight. I stood for a moment outside the revolving door and studied the traffic. It was rush hour, and parking along the curb was prohibited, which made my surveillance easier. No parked vehicles with watching occupants. A few pedestrians, but no bald-headed giants. Taking a deep breath and letting it out again, I started the climb up Tenth Street toward Shockoe Slip.

I kept an eye out as I walked, my focus at first on a fat man stumping toward me down the steep sidewalk, then, after he had passed me, on all the headlights, any of which might turn toward me as the vehicle behind them mounted the curb. As I passed a parking garage, I moved as close as I could to the edge of the sidewalk without stepping in the gutter, fearing the shadowy assailant that might lurch out of the entrance to drag me back into darkness. Then I moved back against the garage, looking up, thinking that someone could shoot down at me from an upper level.

I found myself walking faster and faster, my heart pounding and my mouth dry. The Tobacco

MICHAEL MONHOLLON

Company was at the corner of Tenth and Cary Streets. A tall building with the basement nightclub where I had interrogated Steve Bruno, it had a bar on the ground floor and a restaurant on the second and third. When at last I turned the corner and reached for the door handle, a young man wearing a vest, tuxedo shirt, and black tie opened it for me. I nodded as I went past him.

It was happy hour, and the bar area was loud with talk and music. My muscles relaxed marginally. This was a yuppie crowd: well-dressed men and women in their twenties and thirties winding down after a day in the office. The bar itself, a large square in the middle of the room, had no empty stools that I could see at first glance, but a scan of the stools and of the high tables along the outside walls failed to reveal the man I was looking for. Though a big, bald-headed man wouldn't have been out of place, he would have been noticeable, even in the crowd.

I eliminated the bald-headed criterion and looked again, this time for any tall, heavy men. There were two who would have tipped the scale at two-thirty, and one of them was over six feet, but he looked too much like an accountant and his thinning hair was too obviously his own. It seemed that Mark Walker had not yet arrived.

I stood watching as people pushed past me. A waitress stopped in front of me to ask what she could get me. I waved her off, and she continued working her way around the bar. I got jostled again and saw another waitress working her way toward me.

Heck with it. Wedging myself between two men on stools, standing sideways to the bar, I ordered a margarita from the red-vested, blousy-haired bartender.

"How you doing?" the man next to me said in a voice loud enough to be heard over the conversations going on around us. He was plump and baby-faced and, though it was hard to tell since he was sitting, seemed to be several inches shorter than I was.

"Fine," I said, watching the bartender shake my drink.

"Paul Soldano," he said loudly.

I looked at him, and he smiled at me. He was about my age, thirty, wearing a polo shirt that said Federal Reserve Bank of Richmond on the left breast.

"Mike McMillan," boomed a voice behind me, and I turned to look at the man on the other stool. This one wore a gray suit and striped tie. He was probably an inch or two over six feet, almost tall enough to be Walker, except that he couldn't have weighed over one-eighty or so.

"What is this, a pick-up?" I asked. The bartender set my drink on the counter, and I extracted my wallet from my purse.

The one named Paul beat me to it, laying a ten-dollar bill on the bar. "Only if you want it to be," he said to me.

"I'm meeting someone," I yelled.

"That's okay," he yelled back. He left the ten on the bar. The bartender looked at me and raised her eyebrows. I shrugged and nodded. She took the ten.

"You haven't told us your name," said Mike from behind me.

I stepped back to get them both in front of me. Neither one looked particularly threatening, but I didn't put a lot of stock in appearances. "Do you care what my name is?" I asked.

"It would be friendly," Paul said.

"And you'd like me to be friendly?" I took a sip of my drink. Probably it was a bad idea to have a drink when I was there to meet a man who'd try to run over me, but I was both hungry and thirsty. The tang of tequila and lime juice felt good in my mouth and throat.

"You're not a lawyer, are you?" Paul shouted. When I didn't respond, he rolled his eyes at his friend Mike. "Another one." To me, he added, "Mike's an attorney, too."

Mike grinned. "He's trying hard to be nice. It's the first time I've ever heard Paul use the word attorney without putting the word 'weasely' in front of it."

"I'm honored."

Mike stood up. "Here, take my stool."

I jerked my chin at it. "You keep it." My gaze drifted to the door, then did another sweep of the room.

Paul shouted, "There's more comfortable seating in the back. We can take our drinks."

I glanced at my watch. If there was more seating in the back, maybe Walker was waiting for me there.

"Okay," I said.

"Okay?" The two of them exchanged glances. I had the impression they didn't have much luck with women.

"Let's go on back," I said.

The seating was a lot like it was downstairs in the nightclub: love seats and comfortable chairs arranged around low coffee tables. Surprisingly, given the crowd at the bar, one of the arrangements was vacant.

"Still no Walker," I said, relieved that here it was possible to speak in nearly normal tones.

"What?"

I smiled at Paul and shook my head. The two of them were standing, waiting for me to sit down. They'd left the chair for me rather than a spot on the loveseat. Either they didn't want to crowd me, or they both wanted to sit where they could look at me.

I sat. The chair was low enough that my skirt slid halfway up my thighs. I kept my knees together and pointed to the side to keep the floorshow from getting too entertaining.

"So what do you do?" I asked Paul as I again glanced around us.

"I work at the Federal Reserve."

"So you didn't steal the shirt," I said.

Mike laughed. "He's a bank examiner. Where do you work?"

I told him, and he nodded.

"I'm on my own," he said.

"What do you do?"

"Almost anything."

Paul said, "His bread-and-butter is Social Security Disability."

"That's interesting," I said.

Mike smiled. "No, it's not."

I smiled back and glanced at my watch again.

"Is your date late?" Mike asked.

"He is." He'd said fifteen minutes, and it had been thirty. "He's not really a date, though. He's a potential witness."

Mike's eyebrows went up. "Maybe if he doesn't show up, we can take you to dinner."

"What are you hoping to get out of this?"

"A little feminine company. If you turn us down, it's just Paul and me."

I glanced at Paul.

"You'd be helping us both out," he said. "I'm not much to look at, and Mike's not much of a conversationalist."

"You make it sound really tempting," I said.

Mike took a pull of his beer and set the bottle on the coffee table. "We're what we've got," he said. "How about it? You get a free meal, and you don't even have to tell us your name."

"You two must be pretty hard up."

"Take another look at my alternative there."

I looked at Paul, and he smiled at me engagingly.

"I have to meet someone," I said.

"But he hasn't shown."

"Yes. That worries me." I stood up with my drink. "I'm going to check the bar area again."

Both men stood with me, but sat again as I walked around the corner and back toward the front of the building. The noise level now was terrific, drowning out the background music as I approached. At the edge of the crowd, I stood for a couple of minutes studying the large men in the room, taking a step this way and that to open a line of sight to various points on the opposite side of the bar. I wasn't sure I would recognize Walker if I saw him, but I wanted to give him a chance to recognize me if he were there. No one approached me, though, so I worked my way around the bar, twice excusing myself and pressing between knots of people.

Mike and Paul looked up when I returned. "No luck?" Mike said.

I shook my head and dropped into the vacant chair. Two sets of eyes cut downward. From where Paul was sitting, he could see right up my leg. I rolled my eyes and sat up, putting my drink down on the coffee table.

"Sorry," Paul said. "You've got legs that draw the eye."

"Yes," I said. "It's a burden." Over Paul's left shoulder a door opened as someone came out and someone else went in, neither of them very tall. As the door closed, I could read the word *Gentlemen* stenciled onto the large pane of pebbled glass in the door.

"I wonder if he's in there," I said.

"Your witness?" Paul stood up. "I'll check it out for you. Make it up to you for looking up your dress."

I glanced at Mike as he moved away. "At least he pays his debts," I said.

Mike shrugged. "Paul says what's on his mind. He doesn't have much of a filter between his brain and his mouth."

"I guess there're pluses and minuses to that," I said.

"It can make things interesting."

Paul came back. "Two people in there," he said. "A little blond guy standing at one of the urinals, and somebody sitting in one of the stalls, breathing like he's going to explode."

"What do you mean, 'breathing like he's going to explode'?"

"I mean he's got some kind of breathing problem. A bad one." He sat down, looked at me curiously. "Why? Does your guy have a breathing problem?"

"He didn't forty-five minutes ago. What can you tell me about his feet?"

"His feet?"

"Come on. You're not living up to Mike's testimonial. I'm sure you noticed his feet."

Paul glanced at Mike. "Sneakers," he said. "Fairly new, but I didn't recognize the logo. Faded blue jeans."

"Pulled down on top of the sneakers?"

He shook his head. "I'm not sure. They must have been."

"But you could see the logo."

Paul looked momentarily doubtful. The little blond guy came out of the restroom, and I stood up. "I'm going to check it out."

Mike and Paul stood with me. Mike's smile was incredulous. "What are you going to do, look over the top of the stall?"

"Sure. Why not?"

Paul said, "Because the guy on the pot will see you and raise holy hell?"

"Yeah, that's a pretty good reason," I conceded. "On the other hand, just three-quarters-of-an-hour ago my witness arranged to meet me here, and he hasn't shown." I picked up my purse and started for the men's room. Paul and Mike looked at each other.

Mike said, "That is one compulsive female."

Paul said, "Yes, isn't she great? We can stand guard."

"You stand guard. I'll just kick back here and enjoy the fireworks."

Outside the men's room, I glanced back and saw Mike with one foot on the coffee table and his thumb and forefinger loosely around the neck of his beer bottle. Paul stopped next to me and turned outward, folding his arms across his chest like a bouncer in a bad movie. He gave me a nod of encouragement.

I took a breath and pushed through the door.

Paul was right. No one at the sinks or urinals. A lone pair of off-brand sneakers in one of the stalls. The jeans only reached to the top of the sneakers, which suggested the man was sitting on the pot with his pants up. Even from the doorway, I could hear the rasp of his breathing.

"Hello?" I said.

The cadence of the harsh rattle of breath through the man's throat seemed to increase a fraction, but there was no other reaction. I moved up against the wall of the stall and went up onto my toes. Below me I could see the top of a bald head, bent forward. The head jerked, and the back hitched with each labored breath.

"Are you all right?"

The hitching continued, but the man did not look up.

I stepped back.

"Well?" a voice said behind me, and I whirled. It was Paul.

"I thought you were standing guard," I said.

"I got curious."

"Okay." I put my hand on top of the stall door and shook it. "Hey," I said. "You in there. Are you all right?"

The breathing stopped suddenly. Something hit the side of the stall—once, twice, and then there was silence.

"That's weird," Paul said.

He didn't need to tell me.

He said, "There're a lot of people out there drinking a lot of beer. You don't have much time."

That was true, too. I bent over and looked under the wall of the stall. Though I was able to see that the man did have his pants up, I still couldn't see his face.

"Hey," I said. Still bent over, I located a dry piece of floor to set my purse on. Judging by my admittedly limited observations, there are always puddles on the floor of men's restrooms. My impression is that men only wait to get into the vicinity of a toilet or urinal before taking aim in its general direction. Hands free, I bent down further, putting my hands to the top of my head to keep my hair off the floor.

Despite my best efforts, the top of my head was brushing the floor before I got a glimpse of the face of the man on the pot. What I saw was a fat, swollen neck and a face dark and bloated with suffused blood.

I stood abruptly. "We've got a problem here," I said.

"What?" Paul said. The door of the men's room opened, but it was only Mike.

"I think he's dead," I said.

"He can't be," Paul said. "We just heard him breathing."

"He's dying then." I jerked violently at the door of the stall, trying to shake the bolt free of the lock, but to no avail. Crouching, I considered going under the door on my belly and coming up between the knees of the stall's purple-faced occupant, but didn't like the idea much.

I stood, looking up. The restroom had twelve-foot ceilings, and there was lots of room over the frame of the stall. Reaching up, I put my hands on the top of the frame and jumped. The stall wobbled as I pushed up until my arms were straight and my hips were against the top of the frame. The head below me flopped back, showing an upturned face with bulging eyes and a desperate expression.

"He's alive," I said. I started to swing my foot up to the top of the frame, but my skirt was too tight. I tried again. My skirt rode up on me as I swung my leg, but not enough. "Little help."

"Here," said Paul, behind me.

I felt his hands on my legs, sliding up onto my hips and pushing the skirt with them, and his breath on my bottom even through my panties.

"Thanks," I grunted, though possibly it was a case where helping others was its own reward. I kicked my feet to lose the pumps, then swung my leg up, placing a bare foot on the top of the frame, lifting my other leg over the top of the stall and dropping down inside, nearly catching my chin on the top of the bald head, which again had fallen forward.

"Hey, Mister," I said, gasping. There was no reaction. I put the heel of my hand on his forehead and pushed his head back. His eyes had glazed over, and a thick tongue protruded from his mouth.

I dropped his head and turned to fumble with the catch on the door, pushing at it in a sudden desperation to escape the confined space. On the other side of the door, Paul pushed against me, and the door came open enough to make me remember that I had to pull instead of push. I stepped back, slipped past the edge of the opening door, and tripped over one of my pumps. Paul caught me, cradling me against him. I looked over his shoulder at Mike.

"We've got to call an ambulance. There may still be time."

Mike looked past us into the stall and grimaced. Taking a step backward, he pulled a cell phone from the side pocket of his jacket and slid his thumb over the screen. I recovered my balance and let go of Paul.

"He's choking on something. We can save him," I said.

"How?"

"Heimlich maneuver. He's choking. Help me get him up." We pressed into the stall, one of us on either side of the toilet. I had no idea where to take hold.

"Mike, get in here," Paul called.

Mike appeared in the doorway, flipping shut his cell phone. "The police and an ambulance are on their way."

Paul said, "You're going to have to put your arms around this man's chest and lift him off the pot so she can get in behind him." As Mike hesitated, Paul said to me, "Your arms are longer than mine. As big as this guy is, you're the best candidate to perform the Heimlich."

"Okay," I said.

Mike overcame his squeamishness or whatever was making him hesitate. He took two steps into the stall and bent his knees in front of the man on the toilet, keeping his back straight. Putting his arms around the man's chest, he heaved up and backwards. As the man came up, Paul and I pushed at his back.

Mike staggered backwards out of the stall, clutching his massive burden, and fell. He landed on his back, his head missing the edge of the porcelain sink by less than an inch. He grunted as the air gusted out of him and pushed at the man on top, rolling him off and onto his side.

"Crap," I said. I pushed at the unconscious man's shoulder to roll him onto his back, then straddled him, pulling my skirt up to my hips for the necessary freedom of movement. Mike got up and crouched beside me, the shoulder of his jacket dark with what I hoped was water, since my bare knees were in it. I put the heel of one hand on the man's upper abdomen between his sternum and his navel and put my other hand on top of it. I drove downward, and the man jerked beneath me. I drove downward again. The man's head was back, thrashing feebly. I did it a third time.

There was still no rise and fall of his chest, no sound of breathing.

"It's not working," I said, panting. I rested a hand on the man's swollen neck, which was puffy with air beneath the skin. The sharp point of the Adam's apple wasn't there, but I could feel the hard cartilage at the base of his throat and the indentation above it. "Get me my purse. Do either of you carry a pocketknife?"

Paul opened one and handed it to me. I'd been afraid I was going to have to use my nail file.

"I need a plastic tube. Get my purse and take one of my pens apart." I turned my attention back to the man beneath me. His eyes had rolled back in his head so that only the whites were exposed.

Once, at age fifteen or sixteen, I had seen my father save a German shepherd from choking by opening an alternative airway in its throat. He had jabbed a short, sharp tube through the thin membrane between the thyroid cartilage, which housed the larynx, and the smaller cartilage below it. The membrane, my father told me, had no arterial blood supply and was the only easy place to penetrate the trachea in an emergency. "It would work on people, too," he told me. "The throat's constructed the same way."

Dad wasn't here, and I didn't have a short, sharp tube like the one he had used. What I had was Paul's pocketknife and myself to wield it. I put the point of it against the man's throat, feeling for the indentation above the lower ring of cartilage.

"Do you know what you're doing?" Mike asked me as he unscrewed the pen he had found in my purse.

"Not really." I took a breath, and, with a silent prayer or perhaps just a strong sense of my father looking on, I pressed the point of Paul's knife into the swollen throat, bearing down hard. The knife punctured the skin and sank into the cartilage. I gasped, unsure whether I had killed the man beneath me.

Mike extracted the ink-filled tube from my pen and handed me the lower part of it. I pushed the narrower part of the pen along the edge of the blade as I drew the knife out of the neck. Blood bubbled around the edge of the incision as the air trapped beneath the skin escaped. The man's chest between my knees did not move.

Bending forward, I blew two quick breaths into the tube. I felt a slight movement in the chest beneath my palm. I looked up blindly at the men around me, counting silently: one-hippopotamus-two hippopotamus…When I got to five, I bent down and blew into the tube again, feeling pressure in my face and neck as I tried to force air through the narrow tube, down the man's trachea and into his lungs. When the blowing got suddenly easier, I felt elated until I realized that my own breath was coming back at me around the outside of the pen. I tried to pinch the incision shut and hold it as I blew again.

I gave up, gasping. The tube of the pen was too narrow given the limited amount of air pressure I could muster. What I needed was an air compressor. I got off the man and knelt by his head, thinking. He had been without air for a couple of minutes, maybe more—a couple of minutes going on eternity. I stuck my finger into his neck as I extracted the pen, then shoved another finger in beside it to stretch the incision. It created an opening, something to work with. I inhaled, then bent forward and put my mouth on the bleeding neck. I blew, a long, sustained exhalation that lifted the man's chest, but only marginally. I lifted my head a few inches and felt the warm breath coming up from the gaping throat as the lungs deflated. Tasting the coppery blood on my lips, I put my mouth back over the opening. I blew and saw the chest rise at the edge of my vision. I lifted my mouth and felt warm breath on my face again. I put my mouth back to the neck-hole and blew.

The man's chest hitched on its own. Raising my head, I saw some of the darkness leave his face. There was a faint whistling sound as the man's chest rose. I watched avidly as the chest fell and rose, fell and rose, making a whistling sound as air flowed around my fingers. I pushed the tube back into the incision and extracted my finger. The man kept breathing, the whistle accompanying each inhalation.

"You did it," Mike said, awe in his voice. What I felt was not awe, exactly, but a strange sense of camaraderie with my absent father.

The door of the men's room pushed open, and a man with red hair and a round face came in. He stopped dead at the sight of us crouched around the man on the floor, me looking up at him with a bloodstained mouth.

He screamed, his voice high and shrill like a woman's.

I cringed. "Stop that," I shouted at him.

He stopped screaming and started sucking air as he backed out of the restroom. Mike rose and followed him to the door.

"He's going to attract a crowd," he said. "I'll keep them out until the ambulance gets here." He pulled open the door and went out. As the door closed, I heard him saying, "You can't go in. There's been an accident. The police…" The closing door cut off the rest of it.

The big man on the floor continued breathing on his own, though laboring to do it, his chest working and his head moving spasmodically. The color of his face was returning to normal.

Paul crouched beside me and handed me a wet paper towel. I wiped my mouth with it, and Paul handed me another one.

"Get the phone out of my purse," I said. "There's a girl on the line who's probably calling 9-1-1."

He fished my phone out for me. I jerked my head at him. "Tell her what's going on."

He put the phone to his ear. "Don't call 9-1-1," he said. "Robin is fine. Here." He held up the phone in my direction.

"I'm okay," I called. "Call you later with details."

He put the phone back to his ear. "Okay?" he asked. "Uh oh. Well, we'll deal with it." He put the phone back in my purse. "She already called the police."

"This is going to be a circus."

"Yep. He your witness?" He jerked his head at the man on the floor.

"I don't know."

"Look, his wallet fell out." Using the side of his finger, Paul pushed a long, leather billfold from behind me to where I could see it. He put the back of his fingernail beneath the top fold and flipped it back. A driver's license showed through a window of clear plastic. The picture was that of the man beneath me, though without the pen sticking out of his neck. The name was Mark Thomas Walker.

I nodded. "He's my witness." I got up stiffly and went to the sink. Bending over it, I got a mouthful of warm water, swished it around in my mouth and spat. My next mouthful of water was hotter. I gargled with it, swished, and spat. I got another mouthful of water and gargled some more.

When I turned back to Walker, Paul Soldano was holding up several sheets of copy paper, folded lengthwise and stapled at the corner. "This was in his back pocket." I took the papers from him and opened them. The document was a promissory note bearing the signature of Michael Dillon in blue ink. Michael Dillon had showed me a similar document himself, standing in his living room with Brooke and me while his wife and kids had breakfast in the kitchen. Dillon's copy had been stamped paid, the stamp signed by Mark Walker for Derek Nolan. This one was not stamped paid; if it was the forgery, then Mark Walker must have taken it when he killed Nolan, which made it difficult to understand why he was carrying it around in his pocket.

Abruptly I refolded the paper and reached around Walker to work it back into one of the back pockets of his jeans.

"Useful?" Paul asked me.

"I don't know. Maybe."

"What happened to him, do you know?"

I looked back down at Mark Walker. "Somebody hit him in the throat, smashed his larynx."

"Any idea who?"

"I saw someone going out as that little blond-headed guy was going in, but I didn't pay much attention because I was looking for a big, bald guy."

"So whoever did it was wasn't big and bald."

"And that's about all I can say."

"How did this short, hairy assailant get out of the stall?" Paul asked.

"Crawled out. It's the only way."

"You went over the top."

"Not everybody would have done that. I'm unusual."

Paul nodded, but he said, "I would have said exceptional."

I smiled at him, put out my hand. As he took it, I said, "You've been great. I'm Robin Starling, by the way."

He smiled back. "Pleased to meet you, Robin Starling," he said.

Chapter 22

I didn't get away from the police until nearly midnight. My breaking into a stall in the men's room to perform an emergency tracheotomy seemed to be difficult for the police to accept.

"How did you know to cut into his neck like that?"

"He wasn't breathing. The Heimlich maneuver wasn't dislodging the obstruction. His thyroid cartilage didn't seem to be intact, and whatever he was choking on, he needed an alternative airway, and he needed it quick."

"You know him?"

"I didn't. I know who he is now, of course."

"You didn't go into the Tobacco Company with him?"

"No."

"You weren't there to meet him?"

"I was, but I didn't know it. A man named Mark Walker called me around six and asked me to meet him there."

"A man named Mark Walker."

"But he didn't show."

"He didn't."

"I was having a drink with Paul Soldano and Mike McMillan while I waited for him. Then Paul came out of the men's room saying there was this guy in there having trouble breathing."

"A guy you didn't recognize when you saw him."

"I'd never seen him before."

"You'd never seen Mark Walker before either."

"No."

"I've looked him up. I understand his truck was stolen yesterday."

"I heard that, too."

"After it tried to run over one Robin Starling."

I didn't say anything.

"And today you're slicing open his throat."

"You're talking like I tried to kill him. I saved his life."

"What did he want to talk to you about?"

"He wouldn't say. He asked me to meet him, said he would tell me everything then."

"And you went to meet him, even though you didn't know him, didn't even know what he looked like."

"Yes."

"Even though someone driving his truck tried to kill you last week."

"I'm representing a defendant in a preliminary hearing tomorrow. It's the Nolan murder case. Mark Walker used to work for Nolan. I thought maybe he had information that would help me at the hearing."

"Like what?"

"I have no idea. I had hoped to find that out."

The homicide detective beat a rhythm on the table with his knuckles. I only knew a couple of the detectives, and he wasn't one I had met before. "See, that's what I don't like," he said.

"I don't like it either," I said. "Somebody hit him in the throat hard enough to smash his Adam's apple, and I never got to talk to him."

"Any idea who?"

"No. At a guess, I'd say it was whoever killed Derek Nolan."

"Except that the people who killed Derek Nolan are in jail."

"I'm working under the assumption that they're innocent, and somebody else killed Nolan."

"And that somebody attacked Mark Walker tonight."

"Yes. Somebody at the restaurant. Somebody in the men's room even. I saw a short man with blond hair go in and come out again just before Paul Soldano went in and found Mark Walker. There was somebody else, too, but I didn't get a good look at him. It was somebody short, I think, somebody who was almost hidden behind this blond man."

A corner of the cop's mouth lifted, forming a crooked smile. "Everybody I've heard you describe is short," he said.

"I'm a woman who's five-eleven. A lot of people look that way from up here."

He barked laughter. "Including me, I guess." He held up a hand. "Don't say anything. I don't really want to know." He got up abruptly and left the interview room.

That was the way my interrogation had been going, by fits and starts. I got up to try the door of the room and was almost surprised to find it unlocked. I went down the hall in search of a women's room. When I returned, the detective was standing in the doorway of the interrogation room, his arms folded over his chest.

"Where have you been?"

"Women's room."

"I didn't say you could go."

"My bladder told me I had to."

He grunted. "Come back in here, and we'll try again."

I rolled my eyes, but went back in and resumed my seat.

"Let's go over a few things again," the cop said.

My upper lip rose.

"What?"

"Nothing. It's what we've been doing—going over a few things again and again."

He ignored the implied criticism. "The way I understand it, this Mark Walker was going to meet you in the men's room."

"No, he wasn't going to meet me in the men's room. What kind of sense does that make?"

"It's why I'm asking."

"I told you, I was going to meet him in the bar. He didn't show. I was waiting for him when one of the guys I was with came out of the men's room and said this man was in there. I didn't know it was my guy at the time."

"But you went in."

"That's right. I climbed into the stall. With my friends to help me, we got him stretched out on the floor and went about saving his life. How is he, by the way? I take it he's not conscious yet, or you'd just ask him who attacked him."

"How do these friends of yours come in, this Paul Soldano and Mike McMillan?"

"They don't really. They were at the bar. I chatted with them while I waited for Mark Walker to show. I take it you don't know how he's doing."

The detective made a face. "They've got him on some kind of medication to reduce brain swelling, and they're monitoring brain-wave activity pretty closely. I don't know about the long-term prognosis."

I'd expected better. After a few seconds of silence I passed a hand over my face, taking in a big breath and exhaling it. I felt suddenly more tired than I'd ever felt in my life.

"I can't help but think you have some idea who did this," the detective said. "A guess anyway. However wild it is, I'd like to hear it."

I shook my head. "I don't know anything about it other than what I've told you. Look. It's late, and I've got to be in court at ten o'clock. If you want to go over this again, I'll be right here in the courthouse tomorrow morning. Until then, I'm going home and get some sleep." I stood up.

"Please sit down. We're not quite finished here."

"Or you can charge me with something and put me in a cell, and I'll sleep there. In any case, I'm done."

"You're not in a position to play hardball, Ms. Starling."

"I'm not playing, I'm deadly serious. Why don't you call James Jordan? He knows me."

"Jordan can vouch for you?"

"I don't know. He can at least tell you that climbing into a stall in the men's room isn't that unusual for me."

"Doesn't sound like much of an endorsement."

"I didn't say it was an endorsement. I suggested you talk to him."

The detective nodded, pursed his lips. He looked down at his notes. Finally he looked up and said, "Get out of here. I know where to find you."

I didn't make him tell me twice.

The sky was clear, the couple of dozen bright stars visible over the lights of Richmond looking like diamonds against faded velvet. My car was at my office on the other side of downtown. A ride would have been helpful, but I didn't want to hang around the police station long enough to arrange one and didn't want to climb into the back seat of a police car for the second time that evening.

It was cold, though, and I wasn't dressed for it. I started out with my shoulders hunched and my arms crossed over my chest, my purse dangling from one hand. As I was crossing Marshall Street, a car started up halfway up the block. Headlights stabbed on, casting my shadow in front of me, and I stepped up onto the curb as the car rolled toward me. It was a Toyota sedan of some sort, maybe a Camry. I focused on the license plate, intent on committing it to memory so I could recite it to a paramedic after they scraped me off the pavement and stowed me in an ambulance.

A window slid down as the car came to a stop in front of me. It was Paul Soldano. A hint of stubble darkened the lower part of his face, looking odd on the rounded features. "Hey," he said. "I hung around in case you needed a ride."

I exhaled as the tension left me, but exhaustion seemed to enter me along with the next intake of air. "Where's Mike?" I asked.

"He went home. He's got an eight o'clock hearing. Also, he thought we'd missed you."

"I'm all in," I said. "If this is some sort of approach, your timing is way off."

He held his hands up where I could see them. "I'm offering you a ride to your car because you look like you need one. That's all it is."

I nodded, but my mouth was pursed suspiciously. "I may not look it," I said, "but if the party gets rough, I can be a pretty nasty customer."

He laughed. "Oh, you look it. Mike says you could tie a guy in a knot and slam-dunk him in the nearest dumpster. Not me maybe. Me you might have to roll."

I felt a smile twitch the corner of my mouth. "Mike said that about you?"

"No, I added that myself. You look like you're freezing. Get in."

I nodded jerkily and pulled open the car door. "I think you've got to go up to 12th before you can turn right," I said.

"Got you." He turned on 12th. Past Broad Street Road, the street changed names and curved left around the governor's mansion. We doglegged back to 12th on Bank Street, which ran along the south side of Capitol Square. I had a glimpse up the sloping lawn to the white columns and the pitched roof of the capitol building Thomas Jefferson had designed.

I glanced over at Paul. "How did you make out with the police?"

"Fine. I simplified things a little, told them I heard the guy choking when I went to the restroom, came out and got you and Mike."

I nodded. "Actually, I think that's the way I told it, too."

Paul glanced at me as he turned the corner. "Great minds think alike. Who do you think attacked him?"

"I don't know. My guess would be the partner he had with him a few nights ago when he broke into my house, but I don't know who that was."

"This Mark Walker broke into your house? Did you report it?"

"Sure."

"No wonder the police kept you so long."

"No wonder. His partner had small feet and wore Reeboks, but that's all I know."

"Sounds like a story. Which way?"

"Straight on through the light." I pointed. "When you get to that office building, turn right. My parking garage is right next to it."

He nodded.

"When did the police let you go?" I asked him.

"A bit ago. About ten-thirty."

I glanced at my watch and felt my eyebrows rise. He'd been waiting over an hour.

"What else have I got to do?" he asked rhetorically. "It's not like I have a life."

He turned into my parking garage and wound his way up. When he pulled to a stop behind my car, I reached across the console and closed a hand over his. "Thanks. You've been a life-saver."

He gave me a smile. "Paid in full," he said, but when I got out he stopped me with a "Wait!"

I leaned down to look at him.

"Would it be usurious to press a dinner invitation on you at some point?"

"Interest on the debt?" I shrugged. "Give it a week, and try me at the office," I suggested.

I drove home through a city that seemed clean and empty, deserted except for me. When I got there, Brooke's car was in the garage, but the lights were out and the door of her bedroom was closed. Evidently, my call from the police station, as brief as it had been, had been enough to relieve her anxiety.

Light from a street lamp outside filtered through my blinds, providing enough illumination for me to put my purse in a rocker in the corner of my own bedroom and drape my clothes on it as I took them off. In the bathroom, I washed my face and brushed my teeth, then I stumbled toward my bed and slid between the sheets. For a moment the cotton sheets felt cool against my bare legs, then I was out.

I woke to the whisper of my name and opened my eyes to daylight. Brooke was standing by my bed, looking down at me.

"I'm sorry to wake you, but it's eight o'clock," she said.

I jerked up into sitting position, my heart hammering, before I realized I didn't have to be in court until ten. My heart slowed. "That's all right," I said. "I needed to get up."

"Some cinnamon scones just came out of the oven," she said. "I made two for each of us."

"Better and better." I threw back the covers and swung my legs out of bed.

"But I do want a full account of what happened last night."

I nodded. "Over breakfast. Let's get at those scones."

I had skim milk with mine. Brooke had coffee. When she was up getting a second cup, she took a step toward the window and said, "Did you know there's a police car parked in front of the house?"

"What? No." I got up to look.

"Huh," I said. "I wonder if it has anything to do with last night."

"Could be. You were found crouching over the body of the man who broke into our house. In the men's room."

"Men's room probably didn't help."

"With your pen sticking out of the man's neck."

"The police kept harping on that, but the pen's what saved the man's life—if I managed to save it."

"So you don't have any idea who attacked him?"

"That's something else they kept bugging me about."

"Huh."

We ate in silence for a while, each preoccupied with her own thoughts. At last Brooke said, "You're mother called yesterday."

"I know. She got me at the office."

"You didn't tell me your father came to visit you."

I nodded, my mouth full of scone. I swallowed and said, "I try not to think about it." Even as I said it, I recalled the sense of his presence in the men's room the previous night.

"Why not?"

I shrugged. "That bridge has burned."

"What?"

"The ship has sailed, it's done and dusted, it's all over bar the shouting."

After a moment, Brooke said, "The eagle has landed?"

"What?"

"If you're looking for another cliché."

I frowned. "That one doesn't fit."

"Your father made an important small step."

"A giant leap wouldn't excuse his past behavior."

"Was he looking for an excuse or for forgiveness?"

I sipped my milk as I thought about it. "I don't know what he wanted," I said finally. "He said a relationship."

"Forgive us our trespasses as we forgive those who trespass against us," Brooke said. "We used to say that at church."

"No fair quoting the incarnate God."

"We all need forgiveness."

She was beginning to sound as if she were my spiritual advisor. "If you mean me, of course I need forgiveness. I'm a mess. Pretty much my whole life needs forgiveness."

"Anything specific?"

"Now you just want the juicy details."

Brooke grinned and put the last of her scone in her mouth.

"Okay," I said. "I'll think about it. I don't know what I can do, but I'll think about it."

When I left the house, I drove around the block to see if the police car was still there. It was. I felt a twinge of unease, but that might have been a reaction to the eight-foot long two-by-four that had been holding up one side of my front-porch roof since the attack of the mad pickup truck.

I pulled in behind the police car and stopped. The cop in the driver's seat studied me in his rearview mirror. Then he opened his door and got out.

I unrolled my window as he approached. He was a young man with dark hair—no one I knew. "I hate to invite trouble," I said, "but what's up?"

"Are you Robin Starling?"

"I am."

"Could I see some identification?"

I fished it out of my purse. "Is this normally how you begin a shadowing job?" I asked. "You ask the subject to produce documents to prove he's the one you want to be following?"

"He or she, as the case may be," the cop said, taking my driver's license.

"Hey, you're a poet and don't know it," I said, just to fill the silence.

He studied my license, glancing from it to my face and back again, then he extended it toward me. "My feet show it," he said. "They're Longfellows." He gave me a perfunctory smile as I took back my license. "Have a nice day, Ms. Starling."

"Would a copy of my itinerary make it easier for you, or should I just drive slowly?"

"That won't be necessary, ma'am."

The word gave me a turn. I'd lived to be ma'am'd by a cop.

I pulled away from the curb and drove off, watching the police car in my rearview mirror. It wasn't moving. I slowed at the corner and stopped, waiting for it to come after me, but it didn't. Finally, I took my foot off the brake and let the car roll forward. I turned the corner, drove half a block and stopped. A minute passed, and the patrol car didn't show.

Putting the car in reverse, I drove backwards to the corner. The patrol car was still parked in front of my house, and it showed no sign of going anywhere.

I shifted back into drive and drove forward, thinking. If they weren't interested in me, it had to be the house, and that made no sense at all. I checked my rearview mirror and stayed alert to the cars around me, looking for a police car, marked or unmarked, to slide in behind me. There was nothing, though, not even the speed trap that occasionally slowed the traffic on I-64.

Chapter 23

I sat in district court waiting for the sheriff's office to show up with my clients. Here on the day of the preliminary hearing, I had no plan of action and no theory of the case. I'd already said hello to Matt Nolan, who was sitting in the gallery behind the rail. There was nothing to do but wait.

Finally, Steve Bruno and Lynn Nolan entered the courtroom, followed by a deputy sheriff. They were wearing street clothes, but had their hands cuffed in front of them. I frowned. There was no jury in a preliminary hearing, but they should have been uncuffed outside the courtroom.

"How'd you sleep?" I asked them as the deputy sheriff uncuffed first Lynn, then Steve Bruno.

Bruno answered. "About as well as you'd think." He'd always been lean, but his eyes seemed more sunken and his cheeks more hollow than I remembered.

"Will it all be over soon?" Lynn asked.

I made a face. "I'm afraid not. Sit down." They both dropped tiredly into chairs, and I said, "This is a preliminary hearing. The prosecution doesn't have to prove anything beyond a reasonable doubt. It only has to show probable cause to hold you for the crime of murdering Derek Nolan."

"And it's not hard to show probable cause?" Bruno asked.

"No. Especially not in this case, where they've got a staged suicide and the handgun in Lynn's closet."

"What have they got against me?" he asked.

"We'll find out. Hearsay's not admissible in a preliminary hearing any more than it is in a final trial, so we'll get a look at some of the prosecution's major witnesses. It's what makes this rigmarole worthwhile."

He nodded. Lynn was staring off into space and didn't seem to be paying attention.

Aubrey Biggs entered the courtroom, and I sat up straighter. I hadn't expected to face the district attorney himself in the preliminary hearing. Biggs, ironically, was a short man with a puffy face and a full head of curly hair. Though I'd never seen him in court, he had a reputation for being good. "Ms. Starling," he said, stopping at my table and extending a hand across it.

I stood and took it.

"It's an honor to meet you," he said. "I know you by reputation."

"Likewise," I said, though Aubrey's tone seemed more consistent with an insult than a compliment.

The bailiff came in, bringing with him a cluster of people whom I took to be witnesses in the case. I recognized James Jordan and Stephanie Hoard, the cop who had been so irate at not finding Lynn Nolan in Steve Bruno's room at the Berkeley Hotel. Another cop in uniform looked familiar: I thought he might have been one of the responding officers the night of the murder. Also there were Liz Lockard and several people I didn't recognize.

A man with thinning, red-blond hair looked in at us from the judge's chambers, and I had another sinking feeling. I knew the man. He was the court reporter for District Judge Cochran, whose courtroom I had once fled midtrial to avoid arrest.

Cochran came in, and we all stood. He held out a hand, palm downward as he took his seat, and we all sat.

"Are we all here?" Cochran asked. He was only in his mid-thirties, young for a district judge. His dark hair was clipped close, and he had a trendy goatee.

"Aubrey Biggs for the prosecution," Biggs said, standing.

"Good morning, Mr. Biggs," the judge said with a half-smile.

"Robin Starling, your honor," I said, getting to my feet.

"We meet again," Cochran said. Out of the corner of my eye, I saw Bruno and Lynn both glance in my direction.

"Once more into the fray," I said.

"Don't push it, Ms. Starling," Judge Cochran said.

"No, your honor."

"Steven Bruno, will you stand?" the judge said.

Bruno stood beside me.

"You are represented by Robin Starling?"

Bruno looked at me as if he were reconsidering the wisdom of that, but he said, "Yes, your honor."

"Lynn Nolan?"

Lynn stood.

"You are likewise represented by Ms. Starling?"

She said she was.

Cochran told them about their constitutional rights and asked them if they understood those rights. They said they did. "We'll now go on to a reading of the complaint." He read it, charging each of them with feloniously killing and murdering one Derek Nolan against the peace and dignity of the commonwealth. The complaint didn't tell us anything more about the case than we knew already, but it was all part of the dance.

"Because this is a felony case, I will not call on you to plead," Judge Cochran told the defendants, both still on their feet. "This is a preliminary hearing. I will be hearing evidence in accordance with the rules of evidence applicable to criminal trials in Virginia, but the standard of proof is not beyond a reasonable doubt. My job is only to determine whether there is sufficient cause to charge you with the crime named in the complaint. If I find there is, I will certify the case to the appropriate court having jurisdiction and will commit you to jail or let you to bail pending the main trial. At this hearing, you may cross-examine witnesses and may call witnesses on your own behalf. You may also testify in your own behalf, but you are not required to do so. Do you understand the purpose of the hearing today?"

"Yes, your honor," they both said, not quite in unison.

"You may be seated. Mr. Biggs, would you like to make a brief opening statement?"

"I would, your honor. Before I do, let me say that this case has some unusual elements, and I would like for the testimony of the witnesses to be reduced to writing."

Cochran looked at the witnesses in the gallery of the courtroom. "Do you have some reason to believe that one or more of these witnesses will become unavailable before the main trial?"

"No, your honor." He looked at me. "I have reasons that I would prefer not to go into at the present time, but that I think will become apparent as the hearing progresses. I have provided these reasons to Circuit Judge Nancy Robinson and have an order signed by her that the testimony be reduced to writing." He took the document to the bench and then came by my table to give me a copy. This being only my second preliminary hearing, I had never seen such an order before, but it seemed to be in proper form.

"Very well," Cochran said. He gave his stenographer a nod, and the stenographer went after his Stenograph. "We'll take just a few minutes to get set up."

It didn't take even that long. When the stenographer told the judge he was ready, Cochran nodded at the prosecutor. "Mr. Biggs."

Aubrey Biggs went to the podium facing the judge, where he paused to adjust his glasses and smooth his tie. "Your honor, the prosecution's burden in a preliminary hearing is to show probable cause for holding the defendants to answer for the murder of Derek Nolan. The evidence will show that he was killed with a Smith & Wesson .38 caliber revolver, which was found in a shoebox in defendant Lynn Nolan's bedroom. A different gun, a 9mm automatic, was beside the body not far from the decedent's right hand, and a purported suicide note was on the printer of his computer. The 9mm automatic and the note carried Lynn Nolan's fingerprints. The Smith & Wesson, the murder weapon, had been wiped clean.

"The Nolans' marriage may not have been a happy one. The defendant at the time of her arrest was bruised on one side of her face. It is possible and even likely that she was the victim of spousal abuse. The defense may introduce evidence of this abuse as justification for the crime, but it is the state's position that the bruising, inflicted many hours prior to the shooting, does not rise to the level of legal justification. To the contrary, we will show that Mrs. Nolan had taken a lover, defendant Steve Bruno, which may have been the motivating factor in both the abuse—if there was abuse—and the murder itself.

"That's the gist of our case, your honor. The details will emerge as the trial proceeds. I don't think I need to take up the court's time with any more right now." Biggs sat down. As an opening statement, his remarks were pretty sketchy, but in a preliminary hearing there was no jury to sway. The beauty of the statement, from the prosecution's point of view, was that it gave me almost nothing to work with.

"Ms. Starling?" Cochran said. "Your opening statement."

I stood. I had no theory of the case, at least none that I could produce any evidence to support. "The defense will reserve its opening statement until the beginning of its case, your honor," I said.

Cochran nodded. "Mr. Biggs, call your first witness."

Biggs called Officer Justin Taylor, one of the two police officers who were first on the scene. After he had identified himself, Biggs asked him whether, on the evening of October twenty-third, he and his partner had gone to the Nolan residence on Grace Street.

"We did."

"Why?"

"The dispatcher sent us." Taylor had evidently given testimony before. He didn't try to tell us what the dispatcher told him. He didn't say, for instance, that someone at the house had dialed 911 and hung up, that the dispatcher had tried calling back and received no answer. From Taylor's mouth that would be hearsay, because his knowledge was based on what others had told him. The prosecution could establish the facts by calling the dispatcher, but I thought it unlikely that Biggs would bother.

"What did you find when you got to the house?"

"It's one of those old row houses in Church Hill with servant quarters in the basement," Taylor said. "One set of steps goes up to the front door; another set goes down to a separate apartment, which was set up as an office. The front door to the main house was closed, but light was coming from the open door of the lower apartment, and a young man was standing on the steps."

"Do you know who?"

"Yes. The young man sitting in the gallery behind the defense table."

Biggs turned. "Matt Nolan, will you stand please?" He asked Taylor, "Is that who you mean?"

"Yes, it is."

"What did you do next?"

"My partner asked if everyone was all right. The young man said not exactly."

"Those were his words?"

"Yes."

"Then what happened?"

"A woman came to the door and said there was a body."

"Could you identify that woman?"

"It's the woman sitting next to the defendants."

Biggs turned to me with his eyebrows raised, as if this were a surprise to him. "Counsel for the defense?" he asked his witness. "Robin Starling?"

"Yes, sir." I'd expected this, but what really chapped my behind was that Judge Cochran was looking at me as if this were a suspicious development.

"Then what happened?" Biggs asked.

"My partner Reagan McNally and I went down into the apartment, which as I said was fixed up as an office. The decedent was lying by an overturned chair behind the desk. There was a woman standing over him."

"What woman?"

"The defendant, Lynn Nolan."

"Did she say anything?"

"Yes. She said, 'It's my husband. He's killed himself.'"

"She wanted you to think it was a suicide?"

"She..."

"Objection," I said, interrupting as I jerked to my feet. "Officer Taylor hasn't been qualified as a mind reader."

Cochran looked at Biggs, who didn't say anything. "Sustained," he said.

"She told you it was a suicide, didn't she?" Biggs asked.

"Objection," I said again. "Leading."

"Sustained," Cochran said. On direct examination, it is generally not permissible to ask questions phrased in such a way as to suggest the answer.

"Did she say anything about how her husband met his death?" Biggs asked.

"Asked and answered," I said.

Biggs looked at me. "I'll withdraw the question," he said. He went to his table and picked up an eight-by-ten photograph. He handed it to me. The picture had been taken from the side of the desk. It showed the overturned chair, the body with the out-flung arm, the pistol lying on the carpet. I handed the photograph back to him, and Biggs, getting a nod from the judge, took it to the witness.

"I show you a photograph and ask you if this is what you saw."

Taylor took it. "Yes. This shows the position of the body relative to the desk and to the credenza behind it, and shows the position of the pistol relative to the body."

"I'd like to have this marked State's Exhibit 1, your honor."

The court stenographer marked it. Biggs went back to his table and picked up another photograph. He brought it to me, then showed it to his witness and asked him to identify it. This went on for some time. When Taylor had identified nine photographs, and they had all been marked, Biggs moved to admit them into evidence.

I half-stood. "No objection."

My clients looked at me unhappily as I dropped back into my seat.

Cochran said, "State's Exhibits one through nine are admitted into evidence."

"No further questions," Biggs said.

"Ms. Starling, you may cross-examine."

I went to the podium. "Officer Taylor," I said. "How far away was this pistol from the decedent's hand?"

"A few inches."

"From the right hand?"

"Yes."

"One of the photographs showed paper on the printer. Do you know how many sheets?"

"One, I think."

"Did you read it?"

"Not then."

"But subsequently?"

"Yes."

"What did it say?"

Biggs stood. "Your honor, we will be introducing this paper at a later time. It is itself the best evidence as to what it said."

"Is that an objection?" the judge asked him.

"Yes, your honor."

"Sustained."

"Officer Taylor," I said. "How long have you been a police officer?"

"Fifteen years next month."

"In that time, at how many death scenes have you been present?"

He shifted in his seat. "Somewhere between six and a dozen."

"Here we have a man who had evidently been sitting at his desk. He has a bullet wound in the side of his head and a pistol near his right hand. It looks at least superficially like the scene of a suicide, does it not?"

"I suppose so."

"No further questions."

"No redirect," Biggs said. "Call Dr. William Birdsong."

Birdsong was a deputy coroner with the medical examiner's office. After establishing his credentials, he testified that Derek Nolan had died of a gunshot wound to the right side of his head. "The bullet entered the head just over the ear, moving on a flat trajectory, and flattened against the skull on the opposite side of the head. There was no exit wound."

"How far away was the gun when the bullet was fired?"

"More than two feet, probably more than three."

That eliminated the possibility of suicide, though even on day one I'd had no hopes of it.

"Can you tell us when death occurred?" Biggs asked.

"Based on the temperature and the condition of the body, along with the contents of the stomach, I would say between eight and eight-forty-five, probably between eight-fifteen and eight-thirty."

"Did you recover the bullet?"

"I did. Police detective James Jordan was present. I put the bullet in an envelope and sealed it. Both of us signed the envelope across the flap and I turned it over to him."

"Cross-examine."

I crossed to the podium. Biggs's examination had been very brief, asking for conclusions without eliciting any of the facts on which those conclusions were based. Since I was going to be seeing this same witness in the jury trial, I needed to know those facts.

"How did you establish the probable time of death?" I asked.

"Well," Dr. Birdsong said, settling himself more firmly in his chair, "I first examined the body at the scene, beginning my examination at 10:36. At that time, rigor mortis had not begun, and there was no postmortem lividity. Body temperature was 95.4 degrees. Since at room temperature the body would be expected to lose about one-point-five degrees per hour, that would put the death right at eight-thirty — perhaps just a few minutes earlier."

"That seems unusually precise. I'd like to go through each factor in turn. My understanding of rigor mortis is that its absence tells you only that death occurred within the last three to six hours."

"That's correct."

"So the lack of rigor mortis tells us that death occurred no earlier than 4:36 that afternoon."

"Absent unusual circumstances, yes."

"And the absence of postmortem lividity also gives no more than an outside limit on the time of death."

The doctor was nodding. "Four hours," he said.

"So death occurred no earlier than 6:36."

"That's right."

"And when you say the rate of cooling is about one-point-five degrees per hour…"

"It's a range, generally from one degree per hour to one-point-five."

I did a quick mental calculation. "So based on body temperature alone, the time of death could have been as early as seven-thirty."

"That's right."

"And isn't there usually some uncertainty about the exact baseline temperature from which the cooling started?"

"Yes, there is."

"Which would even further expand the possible range for time of death."

"Yes."

He was beginning to irritate me.

"Since the only other factor you referred to was the contents of the stomach, I can only assume that those were themselves conclusive.

"Yes. The stomach was full, and digestion of the contents had only just begun. Death occurred within thirty minutes of eating, perhaps within fifteen."

"Did you have dinner with the decedent, doctor?"

"I did not."

"You didn't call him on the phone and interrupt his dinner?"

"No."

"So you have no independent knowledge of when this last meal occurred."

"No."

"This apparent precision in time-of-death, eight-fifteen to eight-thirty, is in reality founded entirely on hearsay. Isn't that right?"

"Well," the doctor said, looking for the first time uncomfortable.

Biggs stood. "Your honor, we will establish the last meal by independent testimony."

"I'd like an answer to my last question," I said.

"I'm sorry," the doctor said. "Could you repeat it?"

"The range you gave us for the time of death," I said, "is based entirely on hearsay. Isn't that right, doctor?"

"Well, no. There's the absence of rigor mortis and postmortem lividity…"

"No," I said, interrupting. "Those factors would only tell us that death occurred sometime after six-thirty or seven-thirty. The range you gave us is based entirely on hearsay."

"The body temperature…" He trailed off.

"The range you gave us, eight-fifteen to eight-thirty, is based entirely on hearsay," I said.

"All right. Have it your way."

"I don't want it my way," I said. "I want to know why you're trying so hard to hide the basis of your so-called expert conclusions."

"Your honor," Biggs said. "That's uncalled for."

Cochran said merely, "It's not a question, Ms. Starling."

"I have no further questions," I said, but I turned back after taking only a couple of steps from the podium.

"Doctor," I said.

He stopped halfway to his feet, then dropped back into his chair and waited.

"Did you perform a paraffin test on either hand of Derek Nolan to determine whether the decedent had fired a gun?"

"No. I didn't."

"Why not? There was a pistol found at the scene, was there not? Right next to the decedent's right hand."

"Given the range of the gunshot wound, there was no chance that it was self-inflicted."

"He could have fired a shot at his assailant," I said.

Dr. Birdsong didn't say anything. Of course, I hadn't given him a question to answer. I let the silence draw out for a few seconds, then said, "That's all," and went back to my seat.

"Any redirect?" Cochran asked Biggs.

Biggs hesitated, then shook his head. "No, your honor."

"Dr. Birdsong, you're excused."

Dr. Birdsong shot me a black look as he went by me. Then he pushed through the rail and stalked down the aisle to the door of the courtroom.

"Call Sergeant James Jordan," Biggs said.

Jordan came forward. He swore to tell the truth, then took his place on the witness stand. Biggs got his name, rank, and years with the Richmond Police Department, then spent the better part of half-an-hour going through his credentials: B.S. in criminal justice from VCU with a minor in chemistry; postgraduate coursework in ballistics, fingerprint analysis, forensics, and so on; lead investigator at more than fifty homicide scenes. The purpose of all of it was to establish Jordan as an expert in various fields so Biggs could present his conclusions as evidence. Finally, Biggs asked him if he had been to the Nolan house on Grace Street the night of October twenty-third, and Jordan said he had.

"What did you find there?"

"Two police officers in charge of the crime scene in a basement apartment that had been fitted up as an office. Upstairs in the house were the defendant Lynn Nolan, her son Matt Nolan, and attorney for the defense Robin Starling."

Again Biggs turned to look at me, and I began to have the unpleasant feeling that he was gunning for me. As the district attorney for metropolitan Richmond, there was no reason for him to be handling a preliminary hearing in the first place.

"The defendant Steven Bruno wasn't there?" Biggs asked, turning back to his witness.

"No. We found him later that night at the Berkeley Hotel, about a mile from the Grace Street house."

"Did anyone else connected with the case stay at the Berkeley that night?"

Jordan nodded. "Defendant Lynn Nolan and her son Matt. We told them we needed possession of the house for twenty-four hours. They left and went to the hotel."

"Did they meet with Steve Bruno?"

I stood. Jordan hadn't been at the Berkeley. Anything he knew about what went on there was based on what others had told him.

"I don't know," Jordan said.

"Thank you," Biggs said. "I'll explore that aspect of the case with another witness." He turned and gave me a fatherly smile that I didn't like at all, but I sat. "Did you question Lynn Nolan, Detective Jordan?"

"I did."

"What was the first thing she said to you?"

"She asked me if it wasn't true that her husband had committed suicide. I told her I didn't think so, and Robin Starling, Mrs. Nolan's attorney, asked me why I didn't think so."

"Ah, Ms. Starling asked you that." This time I merited only a sidelong glance. "Did you ask whether either of them had touched anything after finding the body downstairs?"

"I did. Lynn Nolan said they hadn't. Ms. Starling corrected her and said Mrs. Nolan had picked up the paper on the printer and read it."

Biggs handed him a plastic bag with a sheet of paper in it. "Is this the paper?"

Jordan took it and looked at it. "It is."

"Could you read it to the court please?" To the judge, Biggs said, "It's relatively brief, your honor."

Cochran gave him a nod, and Jordan held up the paper and read it through the baggie. "'Matt, Lynn, I'm sorry. I haven't been much of a husband or a father. I've become something I never intended to be. I'm sick of myself and everything around me.'"

Jordan lowered the baggie and looked up. "There's no signature," he said. "Not even a name at the bottom."

"Aside from this hard copy, did you find the document on the computer itself?"

"No. It wasn't any of the documents in the menu 'My Recent Documents,' suggesting it hadn't been saved recently. One of the techs did a search in my presence and under my direction for a file containing the string, 'Matt, Lynn, I'm sorry.'"

"What did he find?"

"She. Tara Walters. She found nothing."

"So evidently somebody typed this out, printed the document, then closed the document without saving it."

I objected. "The question calls for a conclusion. Detective Jordan may well be a computer expert, but I don't think his testimony has established that at this point."

Biggs said, "Your honor, the question concerns a matter of common knowledge."

"Then you don't need to ask it," I said. "Also, the question is leading."

"I'll sustain the objection on both grounds," Cochran said, and I sat down, hoping my clients appreciated the masterful way I had kept a harmless bit of testimony out of the record.

"Were there any fingerprints on the paper?" Biggs asked.

"Yes," Jordan said. "We had to use ninhydrin to develop them. On the front of the paper was Lynn Nolan's right thumbprint. On the back were prints of the four fingers on her right hand."

"So the fingerprints you found were consistent with the defendant's statement, after prompting by her attorney, that she had picked up the document and read it?"

"Objection," I said. "Leading."

Biggs asked, "Did you find anyone else's fingerprints on the paper?"

"No."

"Did you find fingerprints on the computer itself?"

"The decedent's and the defendant's."

"By 'defendant,' you are referring only to the defendant Lynn Nolan?"

"That's right."

"Anyone else's?"

"No."

"Where were the defendant's prints?"

"On the mouse and on the Enter key."

"Is there any way to tell when the prints were put there?"

"No, except that none of the defendant's prints was overlaid with prints of the decedent. Other prints were smudged and overlapping."

"Suggesting that he did not use the computer after she did?"

"Leading," I said.

"Does anything about the positions of the prints of the defendant and the decedent tell you who used the computer last?"

Jordan glanced at me. "Not definitely."

"But it's consistent with…"

"Leading," I said, getting to my feet again.

"Sustained," Cochran said.

Biggs rolled his eyes, and Judge Cochran's eyebrows went up.

"Mr. Biggs, the court has ruled," he said. "And you've made your point."

"Yes, your honor. I'm sorry. I was just reacting to the pettifogging nature of counsel's objections."

"Let's save your reactions for the bathroom mirror, shall we?" Cochran said. "Next question, please."

Biggs took a few seconds to absorb the rebuke. "Our first witness, Officer Taylor, told us that a gun was found at the scene," he said to Detective Jordan. "I'll show you State's Exhibit One, and ask you if the gun was in the position shown in the photograph when you saw it."

"It was."

"Did you check it for prints?"

"Not personally. A lab tech named Danny Golden took prints from the gun in my presence and under my direction."

"Did you personally compare those prints with the prints of anyone connected with this case?"

"Yes. There were prints of the decedent, Derek Nolan, on the barrel and the grip."

"Anyone else's?"

"Yes, sir. On the grip were the prints of the thumb and first two fingers of Lynn Nolan's right hand."

"Were any of the defendant's prints on the desk itself?"

Jordan inclined his head. "On the upper right-hand drawer and on the upper surface of the desk."

"Anywhere else on the desk?"

"No."

"Did you make any attempt to trace the ownership of the gun?"

"We did," Jordan said.

"I show you a paper and ask if you can tell me the significance of it."

Jordan took it. "It's a photocopy of Form 4473 recording the sale of a Browning Hi-Power 9mm automatic. The serial numbers match those of the pistol found near the right hand of Derek Nolan."

"This pistol was a Browning Hi-Power automatic?"

"It was."

"Who was the purchaser, according to this document?"

"Derek Nolan."

"Who made this photocopy?"

"I did, from the records in the Bureau of Alcohol, Tobacco and Firearms."

"Move for admission as State's Exhibit 10."

"No objection," I said.

"Admitted," said the judge. There was an interruption in the proceedings while Biggs got the document marked.

"Now, Officer Jordan. You said Lynn Nolan's fingerprints were on the upper right hand drawer of the desk?"

"Objection," I said. "Asked and answered, as well as leading."

"Sustained."

A smile like a spasm crossed Biggs's face. "Do you know whether Mr. Nolan kept this pistol in the upper right hand drawer of the desk?" he asked Jordan.

"I don't." Biggs had made his point, though. The evidence was at least consistent with Lynn Nolan having doctored the crime scene in an attempt to make it look like a suicide.

"What was the condition of the weapon?"

"It had not been fired since it was last cleaned."

"This gun was not the murder weapon then?"

"It was not."

"And it had not been fired in self-defense."

"No."

Chapter 24

Biggs shuffled his notes at the podium. "I think we got sidetracked," he said to Jordan. "Going back to your questioning of the defendant Lynn Nolan. You said that her attorney was present. Where did this questioning take place?"

"In the house above the apartment where the body of her husband was found."

"Did you ask Mrs. Nolan if she had touched anything in the apartment?"

I stood up. "Your honor, this has been asked and answered."

"I'm just providing the context for my next question," Biggs told the judge. "The witness doesn't need to answer it." To Jordan he said, "Did you ask the same question of the defendant's attorney?"

"Whether Mrs. Nolan had touched anything?"

"Yes."

"I did."

I said, "Your honor, this has also been asked and answered."

"Context, your honor." To Jordan: "Did the defendant say that she and her attorney discovered the body together?"

Cochran looked at me. "I think that's a new question," he said.

"It's leading," I said.

"It isn't," Biggs protested. "The witness can answer 'She did' or 'She did not.'"

Cochran nodded. "Objection overruled."

"Did the defendant say that she and her attorney discovered the body together?" Biggs said again.

"Yes," Jordan answered.

"And they had been together continuously from the time they discovered the body until the police arrived?"

"Now that is leading," I objected.

Biggs, holding up a hand, asked Jordan, "Did the defendant say *whether or not* the two of them had been together continuously from the time they had discovered the body until the police arrived?" He turned his head to smirk at me. Though the question was asked in the alternative, I still thought it suggested the answer Biggs was looking for. I knew from experience, though, that there was no point in objecting.

"She said they had," Jordan said.

"Who called the police?"

"Lynn Nolan. She said she called 9-1-1 and hung up. When the dispatcher called back, she didn't answer. Five or ten minutes after that, the patrol car showed up." Phrased this way, Jordan's testimony wasn't hearsay. It was what the defendant herself had told him.

"How long after finding her husband's body did she place this call?"

"According to her, she placed it before finding her husband's body."

"She called 9-1-1 before finding the body," Biggs said. "Did she say how she happened to do that?"

"She said she called because her son's fiancée had been knocked down on the steps outside the house."

"Which steps? The steps leading up to the house or down into the apartment?"

"Down into the apartment. A man named Charles Rogers who was walking his dog discovered the fiancée lying there unconscious."

"Unconscious. Had she been struck in the head?"

"Possibly. Or she might have been pushed and hit her head on the steps when she fell."

"Who pushed her?"

"According to the defendant, she said a man."

"Who said a man?"

"The fiancée. A Melissa Butler."

"The fiancée said that a man pushed her."

"Yes, on the steps leading down from the sidewalk to the apartment office."

"What did he look like, this man?"

"She didn't say."

"Ms. Butler didn't say?"

"Not according to the defendant. She just said a man."

"So we don't know whether or not this man was short and fat..." Biggs leaned on his elbow and looked at Steve Bruno. "...or tall and thin and had a shaved head."

I wanted to object, but couldn't think of any grounds to.

"No, we don't."

"Did you ask Ms. Butler to clarify the point? Did she not get a good look at her assailant?"

"We haven't been able to find her."

"She wasn't at the crime scene when you got there?"

"She wasn't. Evidently, she had just driven off in the car owned by the defendant's attorney."

"Owned by Ms. Starling?" Biggs tone was incredulous.

"That's what Ms. Starling told us. We later recovered the car at the bus station."

"Did Ms. Butler get on a bus?"

"I don't think so. We have a witness who says she was picked up in a car driven by a woman."

"What woman?"

"The witness couldn't give us much of a description."

"From the description the witness did give, could the woman have been Ms. Starling, counsel for the defense?"

"Objection," I said, standing. "The question is leading and calls for speculation. Once again, the prosecution is attempting to argue its case under the guise of questioning a witness. Furthermore, everything this bus-station witness may or may not have said is hearsay. I move to strike the answers to the last two questions."

Cochran didn't say anything immediately. He looked at me long and hard, and Biggs didn't interrupt him. Finally, Cochran seemed to collect himself, taking a breath and shaking his head very slightly. "Sustained," he said heavily. "We'll strike the statements about how this Ms. Butler left the bus station."

"Have you made any further attempt to locate Ms. Butler?" Biggs asked.

"We have. As of this morning, she hadn't returned to her place of employment, a restaurant named O'Riley's, not even to pick up her last check. We've been keeping an eye on her apartment, but haven't been able to pick her up."

"Do you have a description of this Melissa Butler?"

"Yes. According to the defendant Lynn Nolan, she was about five-five or five-six and weighed perhaps one hundred-twenty pounds. Her most striking feature is her red hair."

"You said you've had her apartment under surveillance. Has no one come and gone?"

"Only Ms. Starling and a young woman who accompanied her."

"Can you describe this young woman?"

I stood. "Was Officer Jordan conducting this surveillance personally?"

The judge looked at Jordan and raised his eyebrows.

"No, your honor," Jordan said.

"Then I object to the question," I said. "It calls for hearsay."

"Sustained."

Biggs said, "One final point, Officer Jordan. I understand the decedent was clutching something in his hand when the body was found. Could you tell us what that was?"

"It was a Motorola cell phone."

"Do you know to whom it belonged?"

"It's registered to the AT&T account of Steven Bruno," Jordan said.

* * *

Jordan was still on the stand when the court recessed for lunch. "I have a couple of minor items to clear up right after lunch," the judge told us. "Let's reconvene at two o'clock."

I drove back to the office, stopping off in the lobby to buy a yogurt-granola shake. I knew many lawyers who could barely eat when they were in trial, but it's never affected me that way. I was ravenous and would have welcomed a half-pound cheeseburger and a mound of fries. I went with the shake only because it was more portable nutrition.

I got off the elevator on my floor. "Hello, Jennifer."

"Hi, Robin." She followed the greeting by mouthing something I couldn't make out. I moved closer.

"He's looking for you," she said softly. "I'll send him back."

I sighed, then nodded. "Thanks for the heads up," I said.

In my office I took a seat behind my desk and spooned yogurt into my mouth. I resisted the urge to put my feet on my desk. I was, after all, wearing a dress, and my boss was on his way. Both feet were demurely on the floor when Larsen stopped in the doorway.

"Robin," he said, as if he were surprised to see me. He glanced over his shoulder as he entered and shut the door, which seemed like a bad sign. Since two walls of my office were made of transparent glass, it seemed pointless as well.

Larsen sat and cleared his throat. "I understand you've been in trial this morning," he said. "The Nolan murder."

"I thought I had to at least see them through the preliminary hearing, since they wouldn't agree to a substitution. It will take the judge's approval to get out."

He nodded, but said, "Did you try to get it?"

"Well. No. Not yet."

He continued to nod, his lips pursed. Finally he said, "I received a call from Aubrey Biggs this morning."

That surprised me. "You did?"

"He wanted to let me know that he'd be filing disciplinary charges against one of my lawyers. He says you tampered with evidence at a crime scene and have been hiding a witness."

"It isn't true," I said.

"Why does he think it is?"

"Because he doesn't like the way the evidence is developing. He's told himself this fantasy that makes it all somebody else's fault."

Larsen just looked at me.

"Pete, he's a pompous little jerk. I don't know why he thinks what he thinks, but I can straighten it all out when the time comes. Trust me."

"Why don't you call him and straighten it out now?"

"Because we're in the middle of a trial. I can't draw him a diagram right now without torpedoing my clients' case."

"Then maybe they don't have much of a case."

"Maybe not. Unlike Mr. Biggs, I'm dealing with the facts as they're given me."

"You know, Robin…" He trailed off, looking away.

"Yes?"

He sighed and turned his gaze back toward me. "You're due to come up for partner at the end of this calendar year, but I don't think it's a vote that's going to go in your favor. Ours is primarily a corporate practice, and your career seems to be developing in another direction."

"It's one trial, Pete."

He looked at me.

"Okay, it's my second criminal trial. Out of sixteen. Two trials don't make a career direction."

"They may be enough to derail a career—as my call from the district attorney indicates."

"It's a phone call, and Aubrey Biggs is a gasbag. He doesn't have to prove anything to make a phone call."

"And he can't prove his assertions?"

"He cannot."

Larsen made a face, nodding again. He stood up. "I wanted to give you as much notice as I could," he said. "You've got till the end of January, nearly three months, to find another position. I'll make phone calls for you and write you a very positive letter of recommendation. Let me know what you need."

I stood, too.

He continued, "You're good with clients. You've had some real success in the courtroom. I'm sure you'll do fine."

He turned and left without saying anything else. I watched him go. No response came to me until the door had closed behind him. I dropped back into my chair.

"Son of a bitch," I said.

I called Brooke on my cell phone as I took the elevator in the parking garage up to my car. "Is there still a police car in front of our house?" I asked.

"Yes."

"They think you're Melissa Butler," I said.

"What?"

"They're confusing you with Melissa Butler. That may be why we had the break-in the other night. Mark Walker—and whoever was with him—also thought Melissa was staying with me."

"But why—"

"Because Melissa saw the killer leaving that downstairs apartment."

"So it was Mark Walker."

"Or the other one. Little Feet." I beeped open my car and climbed into it.

"We need to find Melissa," Brooke said. "Without her, you're never going to prove the person she saw wasn't Steve Bruno."

"It's not up to the defense to prove anything, but I get your point. If we can't find Melissa, it's going to be hard to fight the implication that I spirited her away because she could identify Bruno. I've been thinking, though. Maybe we can get the police to find her for us."

"How are you going to do that?"

"Have you been outside today?"

"I got the paper."

"The mail?" I asked, doglegging west on Main to a through-street that would take me north to the courthouse.

"Not yet."

"Melissa has a darker complexion than you do because of her freckles. And her hair's not as full. Why don't you put on some makeup, the darkest you can find, overdo the mascara to change your appearance a little, and use some of that leave-in conditioner that smoothes your hair and takes some of the body out."

"You mean the frizz out."

"Then go out and get the mail," I said.

"That's it? All that makeup just to get the mail?"

"I want the cops to get a look at you when you're not looking quite yourself."

"How does that help you? It makes it look like you've been hiding Melissa."

"Exactly," I said. "But that's okay, because we can prove you're you any time we need to."

She was silent. "All right," she said finally. "I don't see the point, but I'll do it."

Chapter 25

When I got back to the courtroom, Aubrey Biggs was already at his table, going through some papers and making notes on a legal pad. I stopped just outside the rail and stood looking at him. He had the right, even the obligation, to file disciplinary charges against me if he thought I was violating the rules of professional responsibility. I didn't see that he had any reason to call my boss to try to get me fired, though.

He looked up. "Good afternoon, Ms. Starling."

I nodded, but didn't say anything. He went back to his papers. After a moment I went to my table to arrange my folders and pens and legal pads.

Five minutes before court was to reconvene, a deputy sheriff brought in my clients. Bruno nodded at me, but neither he nor Lynn said anything. Then the bailiff came in with the witnesses, who talked in low voices, rustled clothing, and creaked chairs. At last there was enough noise in the courtroom to drown out the scratch of Aubrey Biggs's pen and the flap of his page turning.

The bailiff called the court to order, and the judge came in. He sat, motioned for us to sit with a wave of his hand, and told Biggs to proceed.

Biggs stood. "With the indulgence of the court, we would like to withdraw Detective Jordan temporarily for another witness. We need to lay the foundation for the rest of his testimony."

Cochran looked at me. "Do you want to cross-examine on the testimony we've had so far, or do you want to wait until the prosecution has finished with Officer Jordan?"

"I'll wait."

"Call Sergeant Robert Garry," Biggs said, standing.

Robert Garry was a police officer who had aided in the search of the Nolan residence the night of the murder. After running through the preliminaries, Biggs asked him if he been involved in the search of the Nolans' bedroom.

"Yes, sir. I searched the closet while others were searching the rest of the room."

"Did you find anything of significance?"

"A pistol in a shoebox."

"A pistol in a shoebox?" Biggs repeated. At that moment a woman came through the courtroom door carrying a shoebox. She met Biggs at the rail and handed him the shoebox, acknowledging his thanks with a quick, nervous smile before turning and going back down the aisle to the door. Biggs carried the shoebox to the witness and handed it to him.

"Is this the shoebox?" Biggs asked.

Garry turned it over in his hands. "This is the one. I recognize it, and I placed a small mark on it here." He pointed.

Biggs extracted a pistol from another box beside his table. He took that to the witness, handed it to him, and gave him the opportunity to turn it over in his hands. "Is this the pistol you found in that shoebox?" he asked.

"Yes, sir."

"Could you describe it?"

"It's a Smith & Wesson .38 caliber revolver, the model they call a LadySmith. It's a small-frame revolver that holds 5 rounds."

"Thank you, Officer." He looked at the judge. "I move that this revolver be admitted into evidence as State's Exhibit 11."

"No objection," I said.

"It will be admitted."

After it had been marked, Biggs asked the witness, "What did you do with this gun after you found it?"

"I turned it over to Sergeant Jordan."

"I'm finished with this witness, your honor."

Looking at me, Judge Cochran said, "Cross-examine."

"No questions."

"Recall Detective Jordan to the stand," Biggs said.

Jordan came forward again, this time carrying a manila envelope, and was reminded that he had already been sworn.

"I understand," he said.

Biggs, standing at the podium, said, "Dr. Birdsong testified to giving you a bullet that he extracted from the skull of Derek Nolan. Did you examine that bullet?"

"Yes. It was a 130 grain bullet, slightly flattened on one side."

"Did you perform any tests in an attempt to determine the gun from which it had been fired?"

"We did."

"We've had evidence concerning two guns in this case, the pistol registered to Derek Nolan and this Smith & Wesson. Was either of these the murder weapon?"

"Yes. The murder weapon was the Ladysmith revolver that's been admitted as Exhibit 11."

Biggs looked at me. "Your witness."

I stood, then paused to think for a moment before I went to the podium. Jordan was still holding the manila envelope he had brought with him to the witness stand. Though I didn't know positively what he had in it, I suspected what he had was a picture taken through a comparison microscope, a picture that showed the image of the fatal bullet overlaying one of a test bullet fired through the Ladysmith revolver. Jordan had given his conclusion, and Biggs was leaving it to me to bring out the facts that supported that conclusion.

I looked at Biggs, who smiled at me urbanely. I sighed. "Detective Jordan," I said. "Is your last answer based on comparison of the fatal bullet to a test bullet in a comparison microscope?"

"It is."

"The fatal bullet was undamaged?"

"As I said, it was flattened on one side, but two-thirds of the perimeter was intact."

"You found not just characteristics of the Ladysmith make and model, but individual markings made by this particular gun?"

"Yes."

"Were you able to trace the Ladysmith? Who bought it?"

Jordan opened the envelope and extracted a legal pad containing handwritten notes. I didn't see the expected photograph. He consulted the notes and said, "Most recently, Albert Landwer of Norfolk, Virginia. He bought the gun from a pawn shop some five years ago."

I waited. "Did you talk to Mr. Landwer?" I asked finally.

"Mr. Landwer died three years ago at the age of seventy-two. The gun seems to have been sold in the estate sale."

"To whom?"

"We don't know. His daughters conducted the sale and kept no record of it."

"So you haven't been able to trace the gun to either defendant."

"We found it in Ms. Nolan's shoebox."

"But you don't know who put it there."

"No, though it was in her closet in her bedroom in her house."

"Suggesting that it was probably someone with access to the house."

"Yes."

"But you found no fingerprints on the gun."

"No, no fingerprints at all."

"Or on the shoebox."

"No."

"Did you try to develop them? Did you try ninhydrin?"

"Of course."

"Could you tell us which pair of Lynn's shoes came in the shoebox?"

"Pardon?"

"It's a Kenneth Cole shoebox. Does Lynn Nolan own a pair of Kenneth Cole shoes?"

Jordan hesitated. "I don't know."

I went forward to look more closely at the shoebox. "Does Lynn Nolan wear a size nine?" I asked Jordan.

"I don't know."

"So you can't say for sure that it was Lynn's shoebox."

"It was in her closet…"

"…in her bedroom, in her house. Yes, I know. But whoever put the gun there might have carried it into the house in the shoebox. As far as you know."

"I guess that's right."

I looked at Biggs again. He was scratching at his legal pad, and he didn't look up. No doubt he was expecting me to spend the rest of the afternoon on my cross-examination. I didn't want to. Nothing I could elicit from Jordan would help me in the preliminary hearing. On the other hand, it was an opportunity to get details that might prove helpful in the main trial.

I took a breath, released it, and set to work.

Chapter 26

When I got home, Brooke was eating a salad and drinking a glass of white wine. The bottle was on the table. I poured myself a glass and sat at the table with her, for the moment too tired to bother about pulling something together to eat, even if it was just a matter of dropping a couple handfuls of mixed greens on a plate and pouring a little vinaigrette on them.

"You look tired," Brooke said.

"Looks don't deceive."

"Trial not going well," she said.

"Maybe as well as could be expected in a preliminary hearing. Aubrey Biggs has done a good job of hanging the murder on Lynn Nolan. My guess is tomorrow he'll start to work on Steve Bruno."

"Aubrey Biggs. Isn't he the D.A.?"

I nodded.

"The big kahuna himself?"

"That would be the one."

"His office must be pretty scared of you, if he feels like he needs to handle a preliminary hearing personally."

"Yeah." I swirled the wine in my glass, frowning at it thoughtfully. "I'm afraid it's more likely he's got another agenda. Evidently, after Melissa Butler made off with my car, she was picked up at the bus station by somebody who could have been me. Later, she went to her apartment with somebody who was me."

Brooke looked startled. "When…"

"When we went to Melissa's apartment, the police had it staked out, apparently. On top of that, they're doing a pretty good job of showing Lynn changed the crime scene — or maybe staged the crime scene altogether — and of course I was there."

"But it was behind your back."

"It's not something I can bring out at this point."

"So what does Biggs want, you think?"

"I think he's after my license to practice law. He's already gotten me fired."

"Robin!"

I nodded somberly, again studying the swirling wine in my long-stemmed glass. I took a sip and put it down. "I'll tell you about it later. I want to take my run before it gets too late."

The police car was still out front. Whatever it was they were hoping to accomplish, they hadn't given up on it yet. By the time I finished my run, I'd decided I would try to take advantage of their persistence. Pieces of a plan had been stirring around it my mind as early as lunchtime, but only after an hour of running down dark, cold streets had it begun to jell.

"Brooke!" I called as I came in the front door.

She came out of her bedroom wearing silk pajamas.

"How willing would you be to spend some time in jail?"

She didn't answer as she took a seat on the couch in the living room and pulled her legs under her. "I can't say it's at the top of my to-do list," she said finally.

"But you'd be willing?" I was bent over double, stretching my hamstrings, twisting my head and looking up at her through a fall of hair.

"Let's start with a no and continue the discussion from there."

"It wouldn't be under your own name, or I don't think it would. And I'd get you out." When she didn't say anything, I said, "Call Matt Nolan tonight. See if he can recognize your voice without you having to identify yourself."

"Matt Nolan, do you know who this is?" she intoned.

"Sure, why not?"

She sat up straighter. "You're not saying the police are tapping our phone?"

"I hope not, but they may be tapping his. It doesn't matter. Ask Matt to pick you up here tomorrow. Wear the dark make-up, put your hair in a braid, and get him to take you by Melissa's apartment. You spend about fifteen minutes there…"

"Doing what?"

I sat down on the floor and pulled my feet in, my knees wide, feeling the stretch in my groin. "It doesn't matter. Use your imagination."

"Fifteen minutes isn't really time enough for…"

"No it's not," I said, cutting her off. "Better stifle your imagination. Just plan to talk."

She giggled, turning slightly pink.

"Then get him to take you to the bus station. Buy a ticket to Arlington."

"And get on the bus?"

I stood and bent over my feet, feeling the stretch in my hips. I said, "I don't think it will get that far, but if it does, yes, get on the bus and go to Arlington. Spend the night, and if nothing happens, come back the next day."

"What do you think will happen?"

"I think the police will pick you up and ask you questions about the murder of Derek Nolan."

"What do I tell them?"

"That you don't know anything about the murder of Derek Nolan."

"Do I tell them my name?"

"Yes. Insist you're Brooke Marshall. That's important. You don't want to lie to the police in a murder investigation. But you won't be carrying any identification, just a purse and some cash. Leave your driver's license and credit cards here in your sock drawer." I mopped sweat from my face with a forearm. "Are you okay with that?"

"You're giving me a recipe for getting arrested. Of course I'm not okay with it."

"You won't be doing anything illegal, just hanging out with Matt Nolan and going to Arlington."

"I don't see the point."

"Melissa saw the murderer. Because she's not available, the prosecution is having to rely on secondary evidence, but as an eyewitness she's the key to the whole thing. If she turns up, she knocks the prosecution's case into a cocked hat."

"Or seals the case against Steve Bruno," Brooke said.

"Or seals the case against Steve Bruno," I conceded. "The point is, if she turns up, it changes everything."

"But she won't show up," Brooke said. "It'll just be me."

"We're the only ones who know that."

"Temporarily."

"Temporarily may be good enough," I said.

Chapter 27

Jordan was waiting for me outside the door of the courtroom the next morning. "Hi, Robin," he said.

"You seem to have slept well after an afternoon of grueling cross-examination."

"As well as can be expected. Look, I know you had an interest in Mark Walker."

"I saved his life."

"Yes. Well, no. Not really." His mouth stretched in a grimace of pain. "He died last night at MCV."

"He died," I repeated, my morning energy leaking out of me like air from a deflating balloon.

"I'm sorry," Jordan said.

"Did he ever regain consciousness? Ever say anything?"

Jordan shook his head.

I took a breath, squaring my shoulders. I had a trial to do.

"I suppose you realize by now that Biggs is laying for you," Jordan said.

I nodded. "On the plus side, he's showing me a lot more of his case that I expected to see in a preliminary hearing."

"On the minus side, it looks to me like he's got you," Jordan said. Behind me in the elevator lobby, one of the elevators dinged, and Jordan's gaze drifted over my shoulder. "Watch yourself," he said softly, and he strode past me toward the elevators.

"Mr. Biggs," he said, "I've got something for you."

I rolled my eyes and pushed through the doors into the courtroom. With friends like Jordan, I'd need to be careful.

My clients were already there. They looked up at me as I pushed through the rail, then looked away again without speaking. Matt wasn't in the gallery. My father was, though, sitting on the aisle in the third row. We made eye contact, and he gave me an apologetic smile. I gave him a half-smile in return, remembering the German shepherd he had saved by opening its trachea, remembering the night I had tried to save Mark Walker.

I hesitated, shrugged, then turned away and sat, taking the case folders from my briefcase and laying them on the desk. "Good morning," I said brightly to my clients.

"Hello," Lynn said. Bruno only nodded. This was the day, I thought, that the prosecution would go to work on him.

Biggs first witness was a tall, long-faced man who looked a bit like Gregory Peck, but turned out to be a private detective named Mitchell Arnold.

"Did you know the decedent, Derek Nolan, during his lifetime?" Biggs asked him.

"I did. He hired me to watch his wife."

"When was this?"

"Middle of September. September 16."

I glanced at my clients. Lynn seemed to be sitting unusually still, which suggested, possibly, that this was the first she knew of Mitchell Arnold.

"What did you do?" Biggs asked him.

"I watched the house from my parked car and followed her when she left it."

"And did she leave it?"

"Oh, yes. I followed her around for eight days. During that time she went to the grocery store twice, got her hair cut once, got her nails done, and met multiple times with a man named Steve Bruno."

Biggs looked at Bruno. "The defendant in this case?"

"You betcha."

That seemed to irritate even Biggs. "How often?" he asked crisply.

"Every one of those eight days."

"Where?"

"Lots of places. They had lunch at a hamburger place on Tenth Street and breakfast at the Berkeley Hotel. On two occasions, she went into the Berkeley in early afternoon—both times between one-thirty and two o'clock—and didn't come out until after four. They met once at a bookstore, he came to the house. I got lots of pictures."

"Did you report all this to your client, Derek Nolan?"

"I did."

"And show him your photographs?"

"Yes."

"Did the news or the photographs seem to upset him?"

"No."

"No?"

"No. If he expressed any emotion at all, I'd say it was triumph."

Biggs gaze slid to the defense table, then went back to the witness stand. "Do you have the photographs with you?"

"Sure. They're in my briefcase. Can I get them?"

Biggs looked at the judge, and Cochran nodded. We watched Arnold step down from the witness stand, push through the rail into the gallery of the courtroom, bend over his briefcase, and return, carrying a manila folder. Back on the stand, he opened it and extracted two eight-by-ten photographs. "This one here shows them standing together in a bookstore in Shockoe Slip." He passed it to Biggs, who carried it to me and then to the judge. "This one was taken at the house." He handed it to Biggs, who glanced at it.

"Derek Nolan's own house?" he asked.

"The house where Derek and Lynn Nolan lived together."

Biggs brought me the photograph. The resolution wasn't the best: It looked as if it was taken with a telephoto lens at early twilight. The figures were recognizable, though. Lynn and Bruno were standing at the rail of a balcony, him wearing a jacket, her wearing a sweater. Her arms were crossed over her chest, and his arm was around her. A stemmed glass half-filled with a dark liquid was on the rail.

Biggs carried the photograph to the judge, who looked at it and nodded.

"Your honor, I'd like to have these admitted into evidence."

"Any objection?" Cochran asked me.

Lynn and Bruno looked at me expectantly, but I didn't have any grounds for an objection. "No, your honor," I said.

"They're admitted. What numbers are we up to?" Cochran asked his court reporter.

The court reporter told him and marked the exhibits.

"I want to ask you a question or two about this picture taken at the house," Biggs said. "Was Derek Nolan at home on that occasion?"

"He wasn't. When I showed him the first of my photographs, one at a diner and a couple at the hotel, he told me he was going to a convention in D.C."

"Did he say why?"

"He wanted to give his wife and her boyfriend lots of rope to hang themselves with." Arnold grinned. "He said he wanted me to supply the rope."

Biggs went to the exhibit table and picked up the cell phone Derek Nolan had been clutching when we found him. He handed it to the witness.

"Have you ever seen this phone before?"

"It looks like one I gave Mr. Nolan. When they were having lunch at Tony's, the hamburger place on Tenth, Mr. Bruno hung his jacket on a coat tree near their booth. This was in the pocket."

"You took it?"

"I did."

"And gave it to Mr. Nolan?"

Arnold nodded. "It was how we identified the boyfriend."

"You traced the number?"

"Well, yes, but it was even easier than that. You just turn it on, and the name shows for a second. Steve Bruno."

"Thank you, Mr. Arnold. Your witness."

I went to the podium. "So it's your testimony that you spied on Lynn Nolan for eight days."

He shrugged. "Sure."

"And that you stole Mr. Bruno's cell phone?" I asked.

"I wouldn't say I stole it."

"You took it without his knowledge or consent with the intent to deprive him of possession indefinitely?"

He looked momentarily uncomfortable. "I guess you could put it that way."

"Putting it that way, you committed common law larceny. Did the district attorney or anyone in his office promise you immunity from prosecution?"

"Not in so many words."

"But that was the understanding?"

He glanced at Biggs, but only for an instant. "Nobody ever said anything about prosecuting me."

There was no point in pressing it further. He had admitted to larceny, a crime of dishonesty, which might be used to weaken his credibility as a witness when the case got to a jury. Here at the preliminary hearing, though, the credibility of witnesses wasn't an issue. "No further questions," I said.

"Call Stephanie Hoard."

That surprised me. Biggs had already connected Lynn to Steve Bruno in a way that suggested a motive for murder. What more did he want?

Stephanie Hoard came forward, wearing blue chinos and a polo shirt and looking much as she had that night at the Berkeley Hotel. After she was sworn, she stepped up into the witness box and sat down.

"What is your name?" Biggs asked her.

She told him.

"Your occupation?"

"I've been an officer with the Richmond Police Department for nine years."

"What were you doing the night of October twenty-third?"

"I was at the Berkeley Hotel to keep an eye on Lynn Nolan."

"Were you alone?"

"I was in charge of a team of four." She named the other members of her team.

"Did you see Lynn Nolan enter the hotel?"

"Yes. We had about thirty minutes notice that she would be going there, and we were in place when she arrived. She checked in and went up to her room on the third floor."

"Did she stay there?"

"We don't think so. As a result of what a member of my team told me, I focused my attention on a room on the fourth floor of the hotel."

"Who was registered in that room?"

"Steven Bruno."

"Did you know anything about Mr. Bruno at that point?"

"I did not."

"Why were you focusing on his room?"

"It was my impression that Lynn Nolan was inside."

I stood up. "I'm concerned that hearsay evidence is sneaking in by the back door here. Did Ms. Hoard herself see Lynn Nolan enter the room of Mr. Bruno?"

The judge looked at her, his eyebrows raised.

"I did not," she said. "I'm telling you the belief I was acting on when I finally entered Mr. Bruno's room with one of my men."

Biggs said, "She's not introducing an out-of-court statement to prove a fact, your honor, but merely to indicate what motivated her. As we'll discover in a moment, her belief may have been erroneous."

"In that case," I said, "I object to the introduction of the witness's beliefs into evidence. The defendants are not bound by something that was going on in her head."

"Sustained."

Biggs stood looking at me as he thought. "Your honor, I would like to withdraw this witness temporarily to ask a question or two of another witness."

"Any objection?" Cochran asked me.

Biggs said, "She's the one who's objecting to hearsay. We have in court the witness who has personal knowledge of the facts at issue."

I hesitated, then nodded. "Okay," I said.

"Very well," Cochran said, "call your witness."

The man who came forward was Adam King. He'd been the one who went up in the elevator with Stephanie Hoard and Bruno and me. After he had identified himself and said he was in the Berkeley Hotel on the night in question, Biggs asked him whether he was watching the door of Lynn Nolan's room.

"I was."

"Did she leave it?"

"Yes. She went down the hall to the elevator and took it to the fourth floor."

"How do you know?"

"I got on the elevator with her."

I glanced at Lynn. It was hard to keep from rolling my eyes at her naivety.

"Where did she go when she got off the elevator?"

"Room 437."

"What did you do?"

"I stayed in the corridor outside the room until we could get a man positioned in the room across the hall."

"Did Lynn Nolan leave Room 437 during that time?"

"She did not."

Biggs looked at the judge. "I'm ready to recall Stephanie Hoard."

"I'd like to ask a few questions on cross-examination," I said.

The judge nodded, and Biggs went back to his table.

"Did you subsequently enter Room 437?" I asked Adam King.

"I did."

"Was Ms. Nolan there?"

"No, she wasn't."

"Had she left the room in the interim?"

Biggs stood. "It seems to be Ms. Starling who is asking for hearsay evidence now," he said.

"If Mr. King has no personal knowledge of the answer to my question, he can tell us that," I said.

"All right," Cochran said. To the witness he said, "Just tell us what you know of your own personal knowledge, not what was told to you by others. Did you see Ms. Nolan leave Room 437?"

"No, I didn't," King said.

"No further questions," I said.

Biggs stood at his table, short and curly headed. "With the court's indulgence, I will call one more witness before recalling Stephanie Hoard to the stand."

"Very well."

He called the man who had been stationed in the room across from Bruno's. His name was Jack Barnes. He said that he had taken a card-key from Stephanie Hoard, gone to the fourth floor and entered Room 438, directly across the hall from Room 437. Adam King was in the hallway in front of Room 438 when he got there.

"What did you do while you occupied that room?" Biggs asked him.

"I stood at the peephole, looking out."

"Could you see the door of Room 437?"

"Yes."

"Could you see people in the hallway well enough to recognize them?"

"Yes."

"Did Lynn Nolan leave that room while you were watching it?"

"Not through the door," Barnes said.

"Thank you. That's all," Biggs said.

I got up to cross-examine, but decided against it. Biggs had made my point for me, that Lynn Nolan could not possibly have been in that hotel room, and it bothered me. "No questions," I said. I sat, beginning to feel the looming mass of approaching disaster.

Stephanie Hoard returned to the witness stand.

Biggs said, "Did you enter Room 437 after Jack Barnes took his place in the room across from it and before he left it?"

"I did."

"Was Lynn Nolan in that room?"

"She was not."

"Who was?"

"The defendant Steve Bruno and the woman now acting as his attorney, Robin Starling."

Cochran's gaze swung to me. Biggs motive was suddenly clear.

"No further questions," Biggs said.

"Ms. Starling?" Cochran said.

"No questions."

"No questions at all?" Biggs said.

I smiled at him, though I felt hollow. "None at all," I said.

"This isn't the end of this," Biggs said. "I intend to bring this matter before the Disciplinary Board."

"This isn't the place to broadcast your intentions," I said.

"We may end by charging you as an accessory after the fact."

"Your honor," I said. "Please tell Mr. Biggs to shut his stupid mouth."

"Ms. Starling!" the judge snapped. "Mr. Biggs," he said with equal force. "You will address your remarks to the court and not to each other. You will behave yourselves with decorum. And you will stay on point. One more exchange like this one, and I will find you both in contempt."

Aubrey Biggs was getting red in the face, and I found myself hoping for a rupture of the vein that was suddenly visible in his forehead.

"Yes, your honor," I said, turning to the judge. "I'm sorry."

When Biggs didn't say anything, Cochran said, "Mr. Biggs? Do I make myself clear?"

"Yes, your honor."

"Do you have another witness, or are you resting your case?"

"Oh, I have more witnesses, your honor."

"Are you sure you need them? I've got a crowded docket and unless the defense intends to put on a case…"

"Your honor," Biggs said, "not only am I concerned about prosecuting these two defendants, but I have a duty to the integrity of the legal profession. This is a good forum for bringing out certain conduct that is not only a violation of professional ethics, but…"

Cochran was shaking his head. "Careful, Mr. Biggs."

"May I ask a question, your honor?" I said. When Cochran nodded, I asked, "Would it be a violation of professional ethics to squash Mr. Biggs's nose all over his fat, red, uninformed face?"

There was a silence.

"Your honor," Biggs said. "This is exactly the kind of thing I've been talking about. Personal threats to opposing counsel in the courtroom…"

Cochran held up a hand, silencing him. "Ms. Starling, you will be spending the night in jail."

"Yes, your honor. I would like to point out, though, that Mr. Biggs has been doing nothing but threaten me for the last five minutes."

"That's enough."

"I would also like to ask whether the court has already decided this case against the defendants before either side has finished presenting its evidence."

Now Judge Cochran was getting red in the face. "Ms. Starling," he began, and stopped. After a few seconds of breathing through flaring nostrils, he said, "We're going to recess for lunch." He picked up his gavel and banged it. "Be back here at one o'clock."

He got up with a jerk and stalked out of the courtroom.

Chapter 28

Biggs left the courtroom without even a glance in my direction. I smiled at my clients in what I hoped was a reassuring way.

"What's going on?" Lynn asked me.

"Nothing important. They're just making an effort to tar us all with the same brush."

Bruno said, "I'm wondering how long you're going to be an effective advocate for us."

I nodded. "I've begun to wonder the same thing myself."

"Is that some kind of joke?"

Lynn said, "If it is, it's hardly reassuring."

I stood and stretched, making a conscious effort to relax as I turned to look back over the gallery of witnesses and spectators. My father was still there, looking dismayed at what he had just witnessed. James Jordan was just going out, and Liz Lockard was there, looking right at me and sneering. I didn't know when Biggs would put her on the stand, but I thought it would be soon. Still smiling, I leaned over Lynn. "Most of what they're throwing at me comes from your actions the night of the murder, first at the crime scene, then at the hotel where I had to insert myself into Steve's room in your place."

Bruno leaned closer. In a whisper, he said, "It just seems to me that the prosecution wouldn't be bothering with any of it if someone else were representing us."

"Biggs would still file a grievance with the Disciplinary Committee, but you're right. I think they'd leave it alone in your trial. On the other hand, whoever represents you in the main trial is going to need to know everything there is to know about the prosecution's case. Since I'm here, I might as well develop it for them."

I patted his shoulder and nodded to the deputy sheriffs who stood by to take them back into custody. As they were led away, I packed up my papers, slung my purse over my shoulder, and picked up my briefcase. Dad was gone, which disappointed me somehow. I began dialing my cell phone with the thumb of my free hand as I walked down the aisle toward the door of the courtroom. A man stood up and walked toward me along the row of seats. He was short and stocky and wearing a corduroy jacket over a shirt with an open collar. It took me a moment to recognize him: Paul Soldano, whom I'd met at the Tobacco Company.

Brooke didn't answer our home phone. I punched END and said to Paul, "What are you doing here? Don't you have a job?"

"I took the day off."

"And you're spending it this way?"

"It's pretty exciting. Is it always like this?"

I glanced around. Only he and I were left in the courtroom. "Not always," I said. "But I do seem to have a knack for irritating the hell out of people."

"I love it. Can I take you to lunch?"

I took a breath. "I'm pretty preoccupied. And I need to make a phone call."

"I'll walk with you."

I shrugged. As we rode down on the elevator, I tried Brooke on her cell. There was no answer there, either. I wondered if Biggs had taken my bait.

I frowned as I punched off the phone.

"A problem?" Paul asked.

"Or an opportunity."

"Ah. You're an optimist."

The comment surprised me enough to break through my distraction, and I smiled at him. "I wouldn't say that. I'm just making a desperate gamble—or trying to."

"Only an optimist would do that."

"Is a cornered rat an optimist?"

We walked across Broad Street and down Ninth to Travelers', the restaurant in the basement of the house where Robert E. Lee and his family had lived during the Civil War. Though I wasn't particularly hungry, Paul probably was, and I had time to kill. I ordered a cup of soup with a half-sandwich. Paul ordered the whole sandwich. Pete Larsen was sitting on the far side of the room with a city councilman, but if he noticed me he didn't let on.

"That's my boss over there, the one with Councilman Akers."

Paul shifted in his seat so he could see. "I don't know Councilman Akers. Is he the guy with the tan?"

"That's the one."

Larsen's gaze slid over me without pausing.

"He seems determined not to notice you," Paul said.

"He is. I've lost my job over this case. I have until the end of the year to find another one."

"Well, that sucks."

"Tell me about it."

The waitress came with our food. I ate slowly, my mind reverting to how the afternoon might play out, trying to anticipate everything that might happen and what I would do if it did. Paul, to his credit, didn't try to fill the silence with a lot of chatter. He seemed content to eat his food and look at me, which I would have expected to make me uncomfortable, but didn't.

I was the one who broke the silence. "In a preliminary hearing, the judge has the power to separate the witnesses, but he doesn't have to."

Paul nodded. "What does that mean?"

"He can keep them out of the courtroom and away from each other, then bring them each into the courtroom when it's their turn to testify. This judge is letting them all sit in the courtroom together."

Again, Paul nodded.

"I think the prosecution allowed it because the witnesses are all his. They can listen to each other and—possibly—coordinate their testimonies, making little adjustments so that the prosecution's case is a consistent whole."

"Could you have objected?"

"Sure."

"Why didn't you?"

"I don't know. A hunch. With any luck it may do me some good this afternoon."

"You want them all in the same courtroom?"

I nodded.

"So you can see their reactions to the testimony?"

"Yes."

"You're not thinking that one of them will leap from his seat, tear open his shirt and shout his confession, are you?"

I smiled. "One can always hope," I said.

At a quarter to one, I said, "I've got to get back."

Paul got up, dropped a twenty on the table, and walked with me back to the courthouse.

A reporter for the *Richmond Times-Dispatch* was waiting outside the door of the courtroom. He and I had gone to the same college, and I knew him vaguely.

"Robin Starling!" he said when he saw me.

"Hi, Blake," I said resignedly. Paul went on into the courtroom, giving no sign that we'd done any more than ride up in the elevator together.

Blake said, "The word is the judge is threatening you with jail time, and Biggs is going to bring you up before the state bar."

I curled my lip at him, trying for a smile. "Who's the source of this word?" I asked.

He laughed as if it were funny. "I can't reveal my sources; you know that."

"So this word is not for attribution," I said, moving away from the door and the people going through it. He stayed with me.

"Exactly," he said.

"And you're going to respect that."

"Absolutely."

I glanced casually around, judging myself out of earshot of everybody but Blake. "So if I were to tell you, speaking not for attribution, that Biggs is a pompous little toad who has his head so far up his butt that he can't see anything but a load of crap, you'd report that without revealing your source?"

Blake's smile faltered.

I patted his cheek. "Gotta go now. Enjoy the show." I moved past him and joined the line of people filing into the courtroom. Inside I looked over the gallery, which was filled with spectators and witnesses, past and future. I saw everyone I expected, including my father. Possibly the trial was reminding him of some of my more volatile teenage years.

I took my seat at the defense table, smiling encouragement to my unhappy clients. The judge came in, and we all stood up. When we were seated, he said, "As you all know—or should know—this is a preliminary hearing in the case of Commonwealth versus Lynn Nolan and Steven Bruno. It is a capital crime. I cannot overemphasize the seriousness of these proceedings. Before lunch there were some unfortunate exchanges between counsel and..." He took a breath. "...some unfortunate exchanges between the court and counsel. We will wipe the slate clean as of now. Ms. Starling, I am not going to hold you in contempt for your comments this morning, but from now on you will address your remarks to the court, and you will refer to opposing counsel in respectful terms. Do you understand me?"

"Yes, your honor."

"And you agree to abide by these instructions?"

I nodded. "I will abide by them."

"Mr. Biggs," the judge said, "You will confine yourself to questioning witnesses and addressing the court. There will be no exchange of personalities. You will refer to opposing counsel in respectful terms. You will make no reference at all to whatever actions you plan to take outside of this courtroom at some future date. Do you understand me?"

"Yes, your honor."

"I believe we have finished with the witness Stephanie Hoard. Do you have any more witnesses to call?"

"Yes, your honor."

"Call your next one."

Biggs called the woman who had been at the desk of the Berkeley Hotel the night of the murder. I recognized her. She was the light-skinned black woman who could have been a model. According to her, Steve Bruno had come striding into the hotel about eight forty-five on the night of the murder—which according to Dr. Birdsong would have been fifteen to thirty minutes after the murder of Derek Nolan.

"Is there any particular reason this sticks in your mind?" Biggs asked her.

"He walked right into a bellhop and knocked a suitcase out of his hands as he was putting it on a luggage trolley."

"And what happened then?" Biggs asked her.

"He said he was sorry and went on."

"Did he try to help pick up the suitcase?"

"No, he didn't."

"That's all I have for this witness, your honor." Biggs didn't even glance in my direction.

I went to the podium. The witness—her name was Whitney James—was a very minor witness for the prosecution. It seemed to me that Biggs was stalling for time.

"I see why you remember the incident," I said to Whitney. "Did anything in particular draw your attention to the time?"

"No."

"You say this was about eight forty-five? Can you narrow it down any more than that? Was it a little before, or a little after?"

"I think it was between eight thirty and eight forty-five."

"There's no point of reference to fix it more definitely?"

She shook her head. "That's just my best recollection?"

"Somebody evidently was checking in at the time. It would have been their luggage that the bellhop was putting on the trolley. Is that right?"

"Yes, that's right."

"Is there a record of check-in times in the hotel computer?"

"Yes."

"That doesn't tell you the exact time?"

"More than a score of people checked into the hotel between eight o'clock and nine-thirty. I'm not sure exactly who was checking in when Mr. Bruno came in."

"But you're pretty sure it was in this eight o'clock to nine-thirty window."

Her eyes cut to Biggs, who said, "I object," just as Whitney said, "Yes."

I looked at Biggs, my eyebrows elevated.

"Your honor, counsel has deliberately mischaracterized the witness's testimony. She said eight thirty to eight forty-five."

"The witness has agreed with Ms. Starling's mischaracterization," Cochran said. "Objection overruled."

I said, "Could it have been any later than nine-thirty?"

She shook her head. "I don't think so."

"It could have been as late as nine thirty, but it couldn't have been nine thirty-one," I said.

She smiled, tilting her head, and I found I liked her. "I don't think it was that late," she said.

"But it could have been?"

"It could have been."

"Could it have been as early as seven fifty-five?"

"I don't think it was."

"But it could have been?"

"It could have been."

"What can you say for certain about the time?"

"It was before the police came in and set up their surveillance, but it wasn't immediately before." Her gaze again went to Biggs, and there was something defiant in it.

"When did the police come in?" I asked.

"Shortly after ten-o'clock."

"Thank you," I said. "One other point, which is really a very minor one. Have you ever before witnessed a hotel guest bumping into anyone?"

"Sure."

"More than one?"

"I think so."

"Did any of them turn out to have been fleeing a murder scene? As far as you know?"

"Objection."
"Overruled."
"Not as far as I know," the witness said.

Chapter 29

Biggs called Elizabeth Lockard to the stand. Though she had been sitting in the gallery with the spectators and the rest of the witnesses, I hadn't noticed until then how she was dressed and made up. Somehow, she had worked the hint of a wave into her short, almost brush-cut hair, and she had applied a little make-up to her square face, using mascara to bring some focus to her pale eyes. Her dress looked like a sack on her thick body, but it was pink and had a diaphanous layer over the bodice. She plunked down in the witness chair, and Biggs asked her to state her name for the record.

"Elizabeth Lockard."

"Where do you live, Ms. Lockard?"

She told him.

"What is your occupation?"

"At the moment I'm unemployed."

"Were you employed on October twenty-third?"

"Yes. I was Derek Nolan's office manager."

"Derek Nolan being the decedent in this case?"

"Yes."

"And the husband of the defendant Lynn Nolan?"

"Yes."

"Did you have any conversation with Mrs. Nolan on October twenty-third, the day of the murder?"

"Yes. She asked me about her husband's insurance."

"What did you ask exactly?"

"She asked me how much he carried. I started explaining to her the way their health insurance worked, but she stopped me. She wasn't interested in health insurance."

"What was she interested in?"

"Life insurance."

"What did you tell her?"

"That she should probably take it up with Mr. Nolan, but then I went ahead and told her what she wanted to know."

"And what did you tell her? How much life insurance did Mr. Nolan carry?"

"A half-million dollars in universal life and another million dollars in term life. I know because I wrote the premium checks each month."

"One-point-five million dollars in life insurance?"

"Yes."

"And that was the end of the conversation."

"No, it wasn't," Liz said. "She also wanted to know about Derek's—Mr. Nolan's—retirement accounts. Those came to another one-point-two million."

"One-point-two million dollars?"

"Yes."

"You told this to the defendant?"

"Yes, though the conversation was making me more and more uncomfortable."

"Never mind how you felt," Biggs said with a glance at me. "Was there more to it? Did she have questions about Mr. Nolan's other assets, his notes receivable and bank accounts and so on?"

"No. That was the end of the conversation."

"I see." Biggs shuffled notes at the podium— not, I think, because he was looking for anything, but because he wanted to place a punctuation mark after this part of the testimony. After a moment he looked up.

"Did your employer Derek Nolan tell you anything about a cell phone that had come into his possession?"

"Yes. He said a private detective had obtained it for him."

I objected. "That's hearsay, your honor. This witness can't testify to anything the decedent may or may not have told her, unless it was said in the presence of one of the defendants."

"Mr. Biggs?" Cochran said. "Do you have a response?"

"No, your honor."

"Objection sustained. We'll strike the last question and answer."

Biggs nodded. "When did you last see your employer, Derek Nolan?" he asked the witness.

"The night he was killed."

"Was he alive or dead?"

"Dead. The police were there. I think Mrs. Nolan had gone up into the house." This was news to me. I hadn't seen her at the scene that night.

"When did you last see Derek Nolan alive?" Biggs asked.

"That afternoon when I left for home."

"You came back that same evening? Why?"

"He asked me to."

"When? Before you left the office for the day, or…"

"He called me on my cell while I was having dinner and asked me to come back. He said there was something he wanted to talk to me about."

"Did he say what?"

"Objection," I said, half rising.

"Sustained."

"What did you do in response to that phone call?" Biggs asked. "Did you return to the house on Grace Street?"

"Yes."

"When?"

"A little after eight, I think. Maybe as late as eight fifteen."

"And the police were there at that time?"

"No. This was perhaps an hour before I came back and found the police there and saw the body."

"Did you go in on this first occasion?"

"No. A woman was standing on the sidewalk in front of the house. I noticed her as I was parking my car."

"Did you recognize her?"

"No. I couldn't see her very well, but I thought she was young, maybe in her early twenties. She was just standing and looking down the stairs to the office. I waited in my car a moment to see what she would do."

"What did she do?"

"She started down the stairs. Almost immediately, a man came bounding up."

"What happened to the young woman?"

"I don't know. I didn't see."

"Did you recognize her?"

"No."

"Did you recognize the man?"

"Not then. I do now."

"Who was it?"

"The defendant, Steven Bruno. That man sitting right there beside Mrs. Nolan." She pointed. It was phony drama, but it made the point damningly enough.

"What did you do?"

"I stayed in my car. The man got into a Mercedes convertible parked at the curb several cars ahead of me. I waited, and, when he pulled out, I followed him."

"Where did he go?"

"To Shockoe Slip. He drove into a parking garage just down Tenth Street from the Tobacco Company. I waited until he came out and walked up the street and went into the Berkeley Hotel."

"What did you do then?"

"I waited for him to come out, but he didn't. After twenty or thirty minutes, I went back to Mr. Nolan's office on Grace Street. I'd gotten to wondering…"

"Objection," I said, not bothering to get to my feet. "Relevance."

"Sustained."

"Were the police there when you got there?" Biggs asked.

"Yes."

"Your witness," Biggs told me.

Steve Bruno grabbed my arm as I stood. I met his eyes, nodded to show I understood. I went to the podium and stood looking at the witness for a long moment.

"Ms. Starling?" the judge said.

I nodded. "That's quite a story," I said to the witness. "When I talked to you the next day, you didn't mention going back to the house that night, did you?"

"I don't remember. I don't believe I did."

"When did you tell the police about seeing Mr. Bruno? The night of the murder?"

"I don't remember."

"It wasn't the night of the murder, was it?"

"I don't remember."

"Did you tell the police when they came to your house the next day?"

"I think so."

"Detective Jordan would confirm that if we called him back to the stand?"

"I don't know. I assume so."

"So it took you a little less than twenty-four hours to come up with this story."

"I didn't come up with it. It's what happened."

"You were standing over the body of your murdered employer, and you didn't say anything about having seen a man running from the office a short time before."

"I've said I don't remember whether I said anything about it or not."

"And you only think you mentioned it the next day."

"I may have told them that night. I'm not sure."

I studied her. She had no doubt signed a statement about all this, but the date of the statement

MICHAEL MONHOLLON

wouldn't indicate definitively when she had first mentioned Bruno.

"Did the police contact you the next day, or did you contact them?"

"They came to see me."

"And you were able to place Steve Bruno at the scene of the crime."

"Yes."

"Did Mr. Bruno see you, do you think?"

"I don't think so."

"If he had, and if he were on the stand, I guess he'd be the one placing you at the scene of the crime."

"I don't know what you mean by that."

"Don't you?" I said.

"No. I don't."

"The young woman didn't see you either, evidently."

"No. I'm sure she didn't."

"Though you place her at the scene of the crime, too. For all you know, she went into the office as this man you saw was coming out."

"As Steve Bruno was coming out."

"You can't say whether the young woman went into the office or stayed on the steps. Can you?"

"No."

"It would make more sense for her to have gone in than to have remained standing in the dark in front of the door down there."

"As I understand it…" She trailed off. "I don't know," she finished. "I wouldn't know about that."

"A man named Charles Rogers found this young woman unconscious on the steps that evening. If he said he saw you crossing the sidewalk to your car before he found her, would he be lying?"

Her eyes widened fractionally. I wondered whether it was panic, but Aubrey Biggs was on his feet objecting. "Your honor, this is outrageous. Charles Rogers hasn't said any such thing, and Ms. Starling knows it."

"I didn't say he said it," I said. "I have asked a hypothetical. I want to know whether Ms. Lockard got out of her car in front of the house that evening at any time before the police got there." But Biggs had already sprung my trap.

"Ms. Lockard?" Cochran said.

"No," she said. "I didn't leave my car."

I took a breath and exhaled it, then moved on. "Somebody embezzled money from Derek Nolan shortly before he died," I said. "Isn't that true?"

"It's what he said."

"You don't know anything about it of your own personal knowledge? Didn't you handle the money for the business? Collect money, pay bills, prepare deposits, balance the check book?"

She hesitated. "Yes."

"But you don't know anything about an embezzlement, other than what Mr. Nolan told you."

"I…" Her eyes moved. "No. Not of my own personal knowledge."

"You embezzled that money, didn't you, Ms. Lockard?"

Biggs started to stand, but subsided, evidently deciding to let the exchange play out.

Lockard said, "I did not. It was Mark Walker, the man who ran errands and did odd-jobs for Mr. Nolan."

"So you do know something about the embezzlement."

"I just know what Mr. Nolan said about it."

"Wasn't Mr. Walker a friend of yours?"

"I knew him from work."

"Didn't you socialize with him occasionally outside of work?"

"No."

"You didn't go to the horse races at Colonial Downs with him on at least one occasion?"

"I did not."

There was a thump at the door of the courtroom just then, and someone called my name: "Robin!" It was Brooke's voice. I turned, but the door had closed again, and no one was there.

Biggs had gotten to his feet. He was puffing his chest and smoothing his suit coat against his sides. It looked as if his big moment had arrived.

Chapter 30

Biggs said, "I see our next witness has arrived, your honor."

"Ms. Starling is in the middle of her cross-examination."

"I'm finished, your honor," I said.

"You're excused, Ms. Lockard," Cochran said.

Biggs pushed through the rail and hurried down the aisle. I suppose it would be uncharitable to say he scurried. He pushed open the door and nodded, then turned and came back down the aisle, followed by Brooke Marshall and a police officer. Brooke had her hair in one long braid down the center of her back, and she was wearing her makeup differently — heavy pancake, dark, burnt-orange streaks emphasizing her cheekbones, and a lot of mascara.

"Your honor," I said mildly. "I don't believe this witness is on the witness list supplied to me by the prosecution."

James Jordan had gotten up and followed Biggs through the rail. He was at the prosecution table speaking in low tones, his back to me, and Biggs was shaking his head emphatically. Finally, Biggs said,

261

"She's snowed you, Jordan." He put a hand on Jordan's chest and pushed.

Jordan stepped back, started to say something else, then shrugged.

"Your honor," Biggs said, "this is a surprise witness. She is not on the witness list, but I do not apologize for that. Counsel has known from the very day of the murder that this was a key witness. Police notified counsel as early as the day of the murder that they sought her for questioning. Despite that, counsel has done her best to keep the witness hidden and to deny both police and prosecution the opportunity to interrogate her."

"Your honor," I said, but Jordan was walking by me on his way back to the gallery. I broke off and laid a hand on his arm as Biggs barreled on.

"The witness can be no surprise to counsel," Biggs said. "She was taken into custody only this morning as she sought to leave counsel's home in the company of the defendant's son Matt Nolan. If not for the felonious actions of counsel…" Biggs was violating the judge's warning to abstain from personalities, but Cochran was looking with interest at the witness, letting Biggs get into his rhythm.

"This witness can identify the murderer," I said to Jordan, my words audible only to him under the thunder of Biggs's oratory. "You might want to follow anyone who leaves the courtroom."

He gave me a look, then pushed through the rail and went down the aisle to the door of the courtroom. As I turned back, Lynn Nolan was craning to look at me with a puzzled expression.

I winked at her, just as Biggs paused to take a breath.

Cochran interrupted. "Ms. Starling. These are serious accusations," he said.

"Yes they are," I said. "Furthermore, the accusations were made in open court in defiance of the court's injunction. I move that Mr. Biggs be held in contempt."

"You ought to be more concerned about your own position than Mr. Biggs's," Cochran said.

"I have obeyed the court's instruction in spite of heavy provocation, waiting patiently for this court to enforce its order."

Cochran's face darkened, but he took a breath and let it out. Turning to Biggs, he said, "You may call your witness."

"The state calls Melissa Butler to the stand."

Brooke didn't move until a cop put a hand to her back and nudged her forward. The court reporter stepped forward and raised his hand. Brooke did likewise.

"Do you swear to tell the truth, the whole truth, and nothing but the truth so help you God?"

"I do," she said.

"Be seated."

She took the step up into the witness box and sat down.

Biggs was at the podium. "State your name for the record," he said.

"Your honor," I said.

Cochran said, "Surely you're not objecting to the witness identifying herself."

I surely wasn't. I was merely stalling. "No, your honor," I said.

"Then may I ask you to sit down?" He put some force into the last two words, and I sat.

Biggs said, "I ask you again to state your name for the record."

She took a breath. "Brooke Marshall," she said. Aside from the Nolans and me, I doubted there was anyone in the courtroom who believed her.

Biggs looked hard at her, waiting for her to wilt under his stare. "Are you aware of the heavy penalties for perjury?" he asked her.

Brooke looked at me, and I knew what she was thinking. I owed her big time.

"I'm aware there are penalties," she said. "I don't know specifically what they are."

"Let me ask you again to tell us your name."

"Brooke Marshall."

Cochran loomed over her from the bench. "You're going to have to tell the truth," he said.

"Yes, your honor."

Biggs said, "What is your name?"

"Brooke Marshall."

Biggs took a breath. "Have you ever gone by any other name?"

"When I was little, my daddy called me Brooklyn."

There was a ripple of laughter behind me. Biggs' neck was puffing up like a toad's.

"This is a court of law," Biggs said ominously. "It is not a place for levity."

"Yes, sir," Brooke said. "I'm sorry. I didn't mean to be funny."

There was another twitter, but Biggs ignored it. "Have you ever gone by the name Melissa Butler?"

"No."

Biggs was breathing heavily now. I thought he might be hyperventilating. "Were you or were you not at the Nolan residence on October twenty-third, the night of the murder?"

"I was," Brooke said.

"Ah hah," Biggs said.

It had gone on long enough. I stood.

"Sit down, Ms. Starling," Cochran said loudly.

"The prosecution is cross-examining its own witness. He's browbeating her."

"If that's an objection, it's overruled. Sit down, Ms. Starling."

I sat.

"Were you at the Nolan residence on the night of October twenty-third?" Biggs asked again.

The question had been asked and answered, but under the circumstances I thought I'd better let it go.

"I was," Brooke said again.

"And you witnessed a man leaving the basement office?" Biggs asked.

"No, I did not."

"Didn't he push you down, or strike at you, and weren't you later found unconscious on the steps by a Charles Rogers?"

"No."

I took a breath as I stood again. "Your honor, if Mr. Biggs is going to testify, he really ought to be under oath."

I think Cochran was about to unload on me, but Biggs beat him to it. "This is Melissa Butler, and you know it," he shouted. "You gave her your car to leave the murder scene the night of the murder, and you've been hiding her at your house ever since."

I looked at him, feeling cold dislike. "Prove it," I said.

It seemed suddenly that everybody in the courtroom was talking at once, and Cochran was pounding his gavel. I kept my attention on Biggs. His hands were clenching and unclenching, and I really thought he might be about to rush me. God was not so good, however. Cochran restored order to his courtroom and said, "Ms. Starling...," before breaking off and turning his attention to Aubrey Biggs. "Mr. Biggs, I think you have demonstrated sufficient cause to charge the accused—Lynn Nolan and Steven Bruno—with the offense of capital murder. In light of these developments, it is time you rested your case. I will certify the case to the appropriate court. You can deal with Ms. Starling at a later time in the appropriate forum."

Biggs had more difficulty bringing himself under control than Cochran had had with his courtroom. He stood breathing hard, his face flushed and his hands twitching as the silence in the courtroom deepened. Finally he said, "Very well, your honor. The prosecution rests."

"Very well." Cochran banged his gavel. "This case is certified..."

"I hate to interrupt," I said, interrupting.

"Then don't. I warn you that the patience of this court has worn very thin."

"Do you intend to preclude the defense from putting on a case?"

"Do you mean that you intend to call witnesses?"

"I'd like to start by cross-examining this one." I pointed at Brooke, who was still on the witness stand.

"I didn't get a chance to examine her in the first place," Biggs objected. "She refused to answer questions."

"On the contrary, she answered every question. You just didn't like the answers she gave. If you're through with her, I would like to cross-examine."

"Ms. Starling," Cochran said. "I think it is highly probable that both you and the witness will be facing prosecution over this. Ask your questions, though, if you want to."

I went to the podium. "Thank you, your honor. Ms. Marshall — is that what you said your name was?"

Brooke nodded. "Brooke Marshall."

"You said you went to the Nolan house the night of the murder. Can you tell us about that?"

"You called and said Matt Nolan's fiancée had driven off with your car. You asked me to come and get you because you needed a ride."

"Why would I call you?"

"We're roommates. I've been renting a bedroom in your house for nearly four months."

"So you were my roommate before the night of the murder."

"Sure."

"What can you tell us about the murder?"

"Mostly what you've told me. You hired me to work for the Nolan estate, and I've done some work on Derek Nolan's financial records."

"You weren't at the house on Grace Street before the police got there?"

"No."

"Nobody knocked you down on the steps leading up to the sidewalk from the downstairs apartment?"

"No."

"You didn't drive off with my car."

"No. I did track down a private detective for you after you recovered the car. You wanted somebody to lift the prints of whoever had taken it."

"Of Melissa Butler."

"If that was her name."

"Thank you, Ms. Marshall. That will be all."

A silence had fallen on the courtroom. Both the judge and Aubrey Biggs were staring hard at Brooke. "If I can begin my case in chief," I said, "I think I can clear all this up."

Cochran nodded slowly.

"Call Matt Nolan."

He came forward and was sworn.

"You're Matt Nolan?" I said. "The son of the defendant, Lynn Nolan, and the decedent Derek Nolan?"

He nodded.

"You have to respond out loud so the court reporter can record your responses," I said.

"Yes. I am."

"Do you think your mother killed your father?"

"No. Of course not. He was abusive. He hit her. But she was going to run away."

"Did you spend any time with your mother the day of the murder?"

He nodded, then caught himself. "Yes. I went with her to your office in the morning to talk about divorce. Then I was with her again in the evening from about 6:30 on."

"Until when?"

"Until a man named Charles Rogers knocked on the door and said there was a woman lying unconscious on the downstairs steps."

"Is this Charles Rogers here in this courtroom?"

He was, because I had subpoenaed him. "Yes," Matt said. "He's there on the second row. On the right. Second from the end."

I turned and looked. "Could you wave at us, Mr. Rogers?" I said.

Rogers waved.

"Who was the woman on the steps?"

"My fiancée, Melissa Butler."

"The woman who just testified?"

"No, that was Brooke Marshall. She's helping me—my mother and me—to wind up my father's collection business. She and Melissa do look alike." He fished in his hip pocket. "I have a picture of Melissa and me. We got it taken in one of those booths in the mall." He handed it to me. I glanced at it, then went and showed it to Biggs. Biggs was beginning to look as if he'd been clubbed in the head with a baseball bat, which I have to say improved his personality. I retrieved the picture from Biggs and took it to the bench to give to Cochran.

"That's all I have for this witness," I said.

"Aren't you going to submit the picture into evidence?" Biggs said.

"All right. Can we have it marked please? Defendants' Exhibit One. Thank you. I take it there's no objection?"

Biggs shook his head.

Cochran said, "There being no objection, the picture is admitted into evidence."

"No questions," Biggs said.

I called Rodney Burns.

"Mr. Burns," I said when he had been sworn and had taken a seat. "Could you tell us your profession?"

"I'm a private investigator licensed by the Commonwealth of Virginia."

"Were you so employed on October twenty-fourth?"

"Yes. That was the day you drove up in a red Volkswagen Beetle and asked me to dust it for prints."

"It was also the day after the murder, and the day after Melissa Butler helped herself to my car. Did you find any prints?"

"A lot."

"Some of them mine?"

He nodded. "I took your prints for comparison purposes, but I still had several after I had eliminated them."

"Were you ever able to identify the prints?"

"Yes. They belonged to a woman who was wanted by the Arlington police. Her name was Melanie Burke."

"What was she wanted for?"

"Murder. She mutilated her boyfriend, and he died from his injuries."

"What do you have in the envelope you're carrying?"

"Faxed pages from the Arlington police reports."

"May we have them?"

He withdrew the pages from the envelope and handed them to me. I was glad to see there was a picture—not a good one, but clearly recognizable as the same girl as in Matt's picture. I carried the papers over to Biggs, who leafed through them and handed them back. I carried them to the judge and handed the pages to him.

He took them, frowning. "Ms. Starling, is it your contention that Melissa Burke or Melanie Butler or whoever she is killed Derek Nolan?"

"No, your honor. I won't rule it out, but that isn't my contention."

He held up the papers I had handed him. "Then what is the relevance of these? And, for that matter, the relevance of Mr. Burns's testimony?"

"No relevance. I'm not the one who has made Melanie Burke a central part of the case." I glanced in Biggs's direction. "I would argue, though, that she's no less relevant than she was twenty minutes ago when my roommate and I were being threatened with jail."

"How do you account for her disappearance?"

"Her police record. After Melanie Burke jumped bail, she moved to Richmond, managed somehow to produce whatever documents allowed her to get a job—I haven't had time to explore that angle—and picked up a boyfriend. When another murder occurred, though, and police started arriving on the scene, she decided it was again time to relocate. Bad luck for my clients, since she had seen the murderer and presumably could have identified him and cleared Steve Bruno."

"What made you think she had a police record?"

"She disappeared and never even returned to work to pick up her last paycheck. Something had to account for it. I had one major advantage over the police. I knew I hadn't spirited her away, and I wasn't hiding her. The police and the prosecution were so focused on me they couldn't think about anything else."

Cochran's gaze slid toward Biggs.

"I did hope for one good thing to come of the prosecution's mistake. Melissa Butler, as far as everyone knows, got a good look at the murderer, but it's possible that the murderer didn't get a good look at her. Brooke Marshall and she do look superficially alike. When Brooke Marshall was hauled into the courtroom and placed on the witness stand, the murderer would want to get out."

Cochran looked at Steve Bruno.

"Obviously, if Mr. Bruno was the man on the stairs, he was going to have to face the witness. My contention, though, is that it was someone else. I've had everyone who wasn't on the prosecution's witness list subpoenaed so they'd be here today."

I turned to look over the gallery and with some dismay saw James Jordan standing in the back of the courtroom, just inside the doors. He shook his head at me.

The inside pocket of my jacket vibrated against my left breast, and I jumped about a foot. I fished out my cell phone and flicked it open. "Excuse me," I said to the judge. "Hello?"

It was Paul Soldano. "When that redhead came in, Elizabeth Lockard got up and left the courtroom," he said. "I figured she was just going to the ladies' room, but I followed her anyway. Right now, she's on I-64 heading west. I'm right behind her."

"You're a life-saver. Don't lose her." I looked up. "Liz Lockard has fled the courtroom."

"She seems to be having trouble deciding where to go," Paul Soldano said in my ear. "Are you there?"

"I'm here."

"First, she got onto I-64 headed east, and I thought she was going to the airport. Then she exited and got back on the interstate going the other way. Now she's taking the Glenside Drive exit."

"Probably going home," I said. James Jordan looked as if he was on the point of flight.

"Your honor, could we recess until tomorrow morning? I'd like to go with Officer Jordan when he goes to pick her up."

"Melissa Butler said she was struck by a man," Biggs said.

"Probably she didn't get any better look at her assailant than her assailant got at her. On the other hand, you've seen Liz Lockard."

Somebody in the courtroom snorted explosively. The sound was followed by a nervous titter, and a corner of Cochran's mouth lifted in the start of a smile.

"Can we recess?" I said, already pushing through the rail. "I really want to be in on this."

After the briefest hesitation, Cochran nodded. "Officer Jordan, take her with you."

Chapter 31

Jordan looked at my feet, saw I was wearing flat-soled shoes, and nodded. "Let's go," he said.

We bypassed the elevator and took the stairs.

"How the hell did she get by you?" I asked.

"I don't know. I think she left the stairs at the second floor and either switched stairwells or took the elevator down. How did your colleague manage to stay with her?"

"I don't know."

Jordan's car was just around the corner of the courthouse, parked against the curb. As I got in and pulled on my seatbelt, he took a bubble light off the seat between us and clamped it magnetically to the roof of his car. He slammed the car door and turned the key.

At Broad Street, he turned toward I-64. The siren let us slide smoothly through two red lights, and then we were at the on-ramp. "I missed what went on in court," he shouted over the siren. "Why is everyone convinced Liz Lockard's guilty?"

"Hocus pocus," I shouted back.

"What?"

"The affect is temporary. I haven't proved anything except that Liz Lockard left the courtroom and that I didn't obstruct justice. By now Biggs and Judge Cochran have probably realized it."

He spared me a glance, though the needle of the speedometer was at eighty-five and his hands were rigid on the steering wheel. "Then what are we doing?"

"Seeing what develops. I'm pretty sure Liz embezzled money from Derek Nolan. She framed her boyfriend for it, Mark Walker, who was combination errand boy and handyman for Nolan. I think Nolan figured it out, threatened her with prosecution, and she shot him."

He shook his head.

"I know. It's guesswork. If I were a better lawyer, I could bring all this out in the courtroom."

"If you were a better lawyer, you'd run a conventional trial, and your clients would be convicted."

I wondered if there was a compliment in that somewhere. "Acquittal is still a long shot," I shouted. "I just don't have anything else."

Jordan exited the interstate, went through a light, then killed his siren as we got close to Lockard's house. When we turned onto her block, I saw Paul Soldano's car against the curb across the street from the house. Liz's faded Toyota was in her driveway.

Paul opened his car door as Jordan stopped on the street and got out of the car. Jordan had a big automatic in his right hand, though I hadn't seen him draw it. "You stay here," he said.

He started up the walk, and I was right behind him. He stopped me with a gesture as he mounted the stairs. He made a circling motion with his free hand, which I took as an instruction to go watch the back of the house. I started around, hearing the faint sound of chimes inside the house. Jordan had rung the bell.

The gunshot sounded as I reached the corner of the house, a reverberating *crack* that was immediately followed by two more. I reversed course and ran back toward the front door. Paul Soldano was on the sidewalk, standing frozen. James Jordan was on the front stoop, bent almost backward over the rail, his head in a large bush and his body sliding away from the front of the house. His pistol fell from his fingers and clattered onto the top step and down to the sidewalk. The front door was open about a foot and swinging slowly inward as Jordan fell from the stoop, his shoulder hitting the scraggly lawn with its hard-packed dirt, the rest of his body landing on the sidewalk.

I went by him, taking the stoop in a single jump. I slammed into the front door, bouncing it off the wall beside it so hard that the door nearly hit me as I went through. Liz Lockard lay on her back, so close to the door that I stepped in the middle of her abdomen, lost my balance and stumbled to my knees by a revolver that lay on the rug just beyond her body.

I lunged to my feet, looking down at her. Her open eyes were vacant, staring blindly upward. Blood spouted from the side of her neck and puddled beneath her head and neck. She wasn't dead—the blood spouting from the carotid artery told me that—but she was dying too rapidly for me to do anything about it. I stepped over her and went out the door.

Jordan was down, Paul standing over him with a cell phone. He was giving the address. "There's a police officer down," he said. "He's been shot." At his feet Jordan lay on his side, each breath whistling faintly like a flute sucking air, the front of his shirt sodden with blood.

Dropping to my knees beside him, I ripped open his shirt. There was a hole in the blood-soaked T-shirt beneath it, low in his chest. I forced up the T-shirt so I could see the wound. As the chest hitched upward, air whistled through the hole in the chest wall. The chest didn't fall. Jordan struggled to exhale, but the air wasn't going anywhere. It was going in through the bullet wound, but wasn't coming out again.

"Paul," I shouted. "Get down here and keep your hand pressed to this wound."

I lurched to my feet, stumbling back up the stairs into the house, leaping over Lockard's body, running to the kitchen, jerking open the door of the cabinet beneath the sink. The half-full box of Hefty garbage bags was an answer to prayer. I grabbed it and ran. Jordan's efforts to breathe were drawing air into the chest cavity outside the lung, collapsing it. I had to do something, or he wouldn't survive until the paramedics got there.

Back outside, I dropped to my knees again beside Jordan's body, opposite Paul. I yanked a garbage bag from the box and pressed it down on top of Paul's hand. "Okay," I said. "You can slide it out. Try not to hurt him."

Paul withdrew a hand dripping with blood and wiped it on the grass as I smoothed the black plastic over Jordan's chest, trying to seal off the wound. The movement of air as Jordan inhaled helped to suck it tight. I sat cross-legged on the grass beside Jordan, one hand pressed to the plastic-covered wound, the other grasping his wrist in search of a pulse.

I couldn't find one. Panic was rising in my own chest when I noticed the pulse beating visibly in Jordan's neck. I'd never been good at finding a pulse in people's wrists. On the other hand, if Jordan was in shock, his blood pressure would be falling, and his radial pulse would be the first to disappear.

"Is he dying?" Paul asked, hunkering down next to me.

"I don't know. Something's happening to him." Whatever it was, it wasn't something good. The veins in Jordan's neck bulged as the external jugular veins became progressively distended. His trachea deviated left as the mass of air building in his chest cavity pushed it over.

Jordan whispered something between gasps, and I leaned over him. "What?" I asked.

He gasped and said it again.

"He says he's thirsty," Paul said.

It was the least of his problems. He was gasping uselessly, the veins in his neck swelling, his trachea moving further left with each intake of breath. No air at all was coming out between breaths. I closed my eyes, trying to visualize what was happening. I saw the diaphragm dropping, drawing air into the lungs—and through them, out through the hole in the punctured lung and into the chest cavity where it was becoming trapped.

"I need another tube of some kind," I said, my voice unnaturally loud. I saw for a moment the face of my father in the courtroom, but where was he now when I needed him? I opened my eyes and looked at Paul. "A tube like a glass straw or the body of a pen."

Paul patted the breast of his jacket.

"Maybe a turkey baster or something like it from the kitchen," I said. "Oh, crap. I don't think there's time." The pulse was no longer visible in the swollen blood vessels of Jordan's neck.

Paul stood and fished in the pockets of his pants. He came out with a pen.

"Hallelujah," I said. "Take it apart."

He was already unscrewing it. I yanked the Hefty bag away from Jordan's chest. No air leaked from the wound. The veins in his neck were thick, blue cords.

"It has to be now," I said.

Paul handed me the bottom half of his pen. I put the narrow end against the bullet wound in Jordan's chest. It wasn't sanitary, but antibiotics would have to take care of that later. I pushed the cylinder of the pen into Jordan's chest, following the path of the bullet wound as best I could, getting onto my knees in order to exert more pressure. I was panting.

"Aren't you afraid of puncturing an organ?" Paul asked. It was the first unhelpful thing he had said.

"Terrified," I said.

Abruptly, air whistled through the body of the pen like air from a deflating balloon.

"It's working," Paul said.

The positive effects of the release of air were already evident. The bulging veins in Jordan's neck were retreating, becoming less prominent by the second as air continued to flow through the tube, silently now, but still coming. The trachea moved slowly back in the direction of its customary midline position.

I took Jordan's wrist again, feeling for the return of his radial pulse as he came out of shock. I found it just as the faint sounds of a siren reached us and began to grow louder.

Chapter 32

"You did it again," Paul said. "With a pen. I've never seen anything like it."

"He's still bleeding, and there's a bullet in there somewhere."

"But he's stabilized."

"Your," Jordan gasped hoarsely.

I leaned over him. "Easy, Jordan. You're going to make it."

"You're always…trouble," he said.

I kissed his cold, sweaty forehead. "I know. I'm sorry." The sounds of the siren were louder now. The ambulance turned onto the street, and the sound became earsplitting, then died.

"You got Liz Lockard, or we'd all be dead," I said.

"He was amazing," Paul said. "He really was. She shot him in the chest as she opened the door, and he stayed on his feet long enough to get two shots off."

"One of them got her in the side of the neck," I said.

The ambulance jerked to a stop at the end of the sidewalk, and two women got out, clearly paramedics, though they looked like teenagers. I stepped back as they hustled toward us across the lawn. "He's been shot in the chest," I said. "His lung's collapsed."

One of them was already talking into her portable radio. The other motioned me back.

"There's a woman just inside the house who's been shot in the neck," I said. "She's probably dead by now."

My helpfulness earned me a hard stare. Then the paramedic ran lightly up the stairs and disappeared into the house. A police car pulled up as she reappeared, a second police car behind it. Then a fire truck turned the corner at the end of the block. As the paramedic came out of the house and the two of them bent over Jordan, I took another step away from them.

"What happens now?" Paul asked. "To your case, I mean."

I glanced at him, then looked back at Jordan. "It depends. The gun in the shoebox is the main thing that connects Lynn Nolan to the murder. If it turns out Liz Lockard has a key to the Nolan house in her possession, I think Biggs will dismiss. He'll look like a jerk if he goes forward."

"What happens to the charges he's going to file against you?"

I shook my head. "If Lynn and Steve aren't murderers, then I'm not an accessory."

"And you get to keep your job?"

The paramedics had Jordan on a gurney and were wheeling him down the sidewalk toward the ambulance. I made a face. "Probably not. The publicity I get over this will look like notoriety to Larsen."

"What will you do?"

"I don't know. Hang out my shingle, maybe. Go into business for myself."

"I mean, what will you do for dinner?"

"What?"

"I've got a Clark Gable-Claudette Colbert movie on my DVR. We could pick up some appetizers and a bottle of Dom Perignon and go to my apartment to watch it."

I studied him a moment. "Do you think Mike would like my friend Brooke?" I asked.

"The redhead they brought into the courtroom?" He grinned. "I feel sure he would. We don't have to set them up tonight, though, do we?"

I smiled, thinking of him suddenly as a huggable, squeezable teddy bear. "No," I said. "We don't have to set them up tonight."

Brooke's car turned the corner, slowing as it approached the house. The passenger door opened, and my father got out.

"Excuse me," I said to Paul. I started walking toward my father, but had only gone a few paces before I was running. Dad kept walking, the beginnings of a smile clearing the look of worry from his face. My arms went around him as I slammed into him, and he hugged me back, taking no more than a backward step or two to recover his balance.

"I missed you, Punkin," he said, burying his face in my neck.

"I missed you, too, Daddy."

There were tears on my face, but for the moment I was reconciled with the world.

ABOUT THE AUTHOR

Michael Monhollon took out a semester in college to write science fiction stories and collect rejection slips. His first book sale, a legal thriller, came at the age of 31 at about the time *The Firm* was coming out in paperback. Its sales fell short of *The Firm*'s, though, and he continues to work for a living. Currently, he is the dean of the Kelley College of Business at Hardin-Simmons University in Abilene, Texas.